PROJECT SABOTAGE:

NEW THREAT FROM THE GENERAL

INFILTRATION BOOK 2

BY WILLIAM W. KING

First Edition

White Whale Tales, LLC   www.whitewhaletales.com

BISAC Categories:

FIC006000   FICTION / Thrillers / Espionage

FIC036000   FICTION / Thrillers / Technological

FIC031090   FICTION / Thrillers / Terrorism

Summary:

In the midst of a global pandemic a secret threat lives inside the
walls of ordinary Americans. Discover the new attack from the
General in Infiltration Book 2.

III

CONTENTS

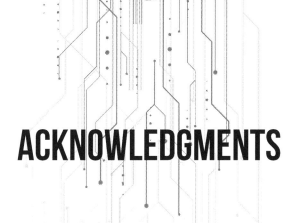

ACKNOWLEDGMENTS

I would like to thank Dr. Linda Tucker, Founder and Editor of Cup and Quill, for allowing me to work with her company in the creation of this book. This novel is my second book and the services of her company have been invaluable. Special thanks go to my editor Dr. Jessica Hammerman for her tireless work and attention to detail through several edits. I incorporated many of her helpful suggestions which significantly improved the plot flow and narrative details. The final product reflects the many improvements she helped me make. Designer and Publisher at Emerald Books, Isaac Peterson, provided the cover design and the expertise for the final publication steps. I could not have accomplished publishing this book without the expert help of Jessica and Isaac, and I greatly appreciate their assistance.

I should add that I am solely responsible for the technical research involved in creating this story. Of course, this is a work of fiction, and the author always reserves the right to stretch the possibilities and the plot, but any technical errors in the narrative are solely my responsibility. Hopefully, I did not make any egregious errors in my effort to write an entertaining story, and I hope the reader finds it to be enjoyable and thought provoking.

DISCLAIMER

This is a work of fiction. Names, characters, business events, plots, and incidents are the product of the author's imagination. Any resemblance to actual persons living or dead, actual companies or products, or actual events is purely coincidental. The plot is a total figment of the author's perverse and highly creative imagination.

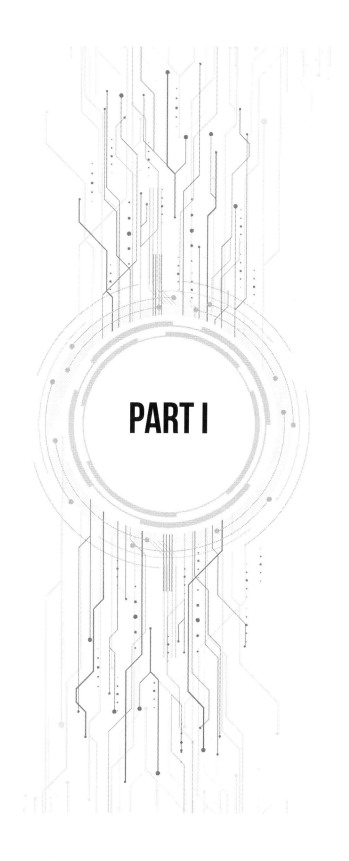

PART I

CHAPTER ONE

FEBRUARY 2020

Julia Tucker had been working at Alligator Enterprises, LLC, in Mountain View, California, for more than a year. So far, she was finding her job satisfactory, though a bit tedious. Alligator's founders selected the unusual name because they were both born in Florida and they imagined that it conveyed an image of toughness and durability. In fact, the company manufactured and sold internet security appliances, so the name had little to do with their products—however, it was probably too late to change it. Besides, they had invested a lot in the design of their company logo—a cutesy, stylized cartoonish green alligator figure holding a lantern.

Now in her early thirties, Julia regretted the fact that she'd dropped out of high school because pregnancy had forced her to support herself and her young daughter as a single mom. She realized that she had severely limited her career choices, and she often thought about how she might fix that problem. Perhaps she would go back to school and earn her GED. That would certainly be a good start.

PROJECT SABOTAGE

The company had recently gone through some layoffs, so at the moment, she was just thankful to have a steady job. Some of her co-workers who had been released were still un-employed, most noticeably those over fifty. Age discrimination was rampant in the Silicon Valley, and some of these individuals probably wouldn't be able to find new jobs locally.

Julia was the lobby receptionist, and she was also tasked with a variety of other assignments, including answering calls and word processing for executives and engineers. She was also tasked with opening and distributing the mail. The lobby was modestly appointed, containing only her small desk, some potted plants in front of the picture windows, and four uphol-stered chairs. The walls were decorated with prints of some of the company's products. Hanging on the wall behind her desk was a large, green 3D representation of the green cartoony alligator just in case a visitor forgot where they were.

This morning, there were no visitors in the lobby nor any other employees. Julia was sitting at her computer scrolling the latest reports about the COVID-19 pandemic that was just beginning to take hold. She was concerned because Santa Clara County had become a local hot spot, and she was quite worried that she or her daughter might become infected. As she gazed across the lobby lost in thought, her eyes fell on the small stack of packages that had been delivered earlier by UPS.

I guess it's time to look at those packages. They aren't going to take care of themselves, she thought, rolling her eyes even though there wasn't anyone there to observe her reaction.

The first package she examined was too heavy for her to lift, but she determined from the label that it contained reams of copier paper. *I'll have someone from the back office come down and move that box to the office supply closet.*

The next box appeared to contain some paperwork addressed to one of the executives. That would be simple—just call his administrative aide and have her come to the lobby and pick it up.

The third box was a puzzle. She set it on her desk to look at it more closely. It was addressed to Alligator Enterprises, but had no return address nor any labels. It was just an unmarked and unremarkable cardboard box about ten inches on a side sealed on the top by a strip of Mylar shipping tape. It didn't occur to her that it might be dangerous, so she concluded that she needed to open it to determine its contents. She grabbed a box cutter from her desk drawer, sliced open the sealing tape, and opened the box flaps.

She shrieked some choice curse words and lurched backward, almost falling out of her chair. Out of the opened box, dozens of cockroaches had sprung out and were scurrying across her desk and crawling down the sides—or in some cases *jumping* to the floor. Two of them crawled onto her blouse sleeve, which threw her into a total panic. She brushed them off with her hand and shuddered in disgust. Before she knew it, they'd managed to run in all directions, and many fled out through the lobby doors into the hallway that led to the building's center. Some were also crawling up the walls and moving into the ceiling spaces above the lobby. There was no way for her to stop them—not that she would have anyway, since she was deathly afraid of cockroaches and couldn't stand the thought of actually touching them.

Where did they come from? Who sent them? What should I do about them now that they are loose? Her first guess was that it was a cruel prank, some sick practical joke. She immediately jumped to the conclusion that it was probably done by a disgruntled laid-off employee. But she had no proof, and it didn't really matter because the cockroaches were here and loose in the building. The priority was to deal with them rather than waste time trying to figure out who the prankster was.

Julia called Derek Jonason, the security manager. "You guys aren't going to believe what just happened. We have a cockroach infestation! I need your help." With increasing panic in her voice, she described what had just occurred.

After listening to her story, Derek lamely replied, "Why are you calling us? We aren't pest control people. You should call the landlord and insist that they fix the problem."

Her voice was getting louder. "Okay, Derek. I'll get in touch with the landlord right away. However, I called you because this is a security issue. The cockroaches arrived this morning in an unlabeled box that was delivered to the lobby. I think someone is pranking us. It might be a former employee."

"I see. Where are the bugs right now?"

Julia sounded like she was on the verge of hysteria. "I have no idea. They've scattered everywhere. There's no telling where they are."

"How many are we talking about?"

Julia replied with a touch of sarcasm. "I, um, didn't think to count them. They were moving so quickly I couldn't have anyway."

Later that day, an inspector showed up from GetOuttaHere Pest Control Company of Sunnyvale. He introduced himself as John Goodbody; Julia contacted security to arrange for an escort. About ten minutes later, Derek entered the lobby.

Goodbody was a pale, heavy-set, middle-aged man with salt-and-pepper long hair in jeans and a blue denim shirt emblazoned with the company logo above his name that was embroidered on the shirt with black thread. Obviously, he'd worked at GetOuttaHere Pest Control Company at least long enough to earn a customized shirt. He was carrying a large briefcase that apparently contained the tools of his trade. Derek noticed that John had a few odd facial tics which might be a sign that he had worked around pesticides for too long.

"Have you had experience dealing with cockroaches?" Derek asked.

John flashed a friendly smile. "Yes, quite a bit. I've been in this business about fifteen years, so I guess I've seen it all."

Derek smiled back. "I bet you have. Where would you like to start?"

John looked around as if this was a difficult question. "The best place to look first is probably the break room. Cockroaches have voracious appetites and will be attracted to the food odors. We'll start with some glue traps and solid poison. People don't like it when you spray chemicals everywhere, so we'll save that for later. Usually the glue traps and edible poison baits are enough."

Derek nodded. "Julia thinks we're dealing with dozens of them. How can we be sure to eliminate all of them?"

Again, John looked around as if this required deep thought. "Well, our first set of bait traps and poison should kill most of them. But you're right, cockroaches are sometimes difficult to get rid of. Later if we see evidence that they're still here, we can try the traps and poison again or do some insecticide spraying."

Derek felt compelled to ask another question. "What do you mean by *evidence*?"

John's face lit up with a broad smile because they had ventured into his area of expertise. "Cockroach infestations are pretty easy to detect. There are several signs that reveal their presence. One is that you will find small brown pellets resembling coffee grounds. You might also find small brown objects that are egg sacks hidden here and there. We need to get rid of them quickly before they lay eggs because that could lead to a major infestation."

John proceeded to place glue traps and poison pellets in key locations throughout the building—in the break rooms, on the floor behind office equipment, and in secluded corners. He looked pleased with himself as he left through the lobby. "Hopefully that'll take care of it. I'll be back in tomorrow. In the meantime, if anyone notices any of 'em trapped on the glue boards or any dead ones around, just, uh, clean them up. Thanks."

CHAPTER TWO

John returned the next day to survey the results. Derek came out to meet him. "How'd we do? Did we get rid of them?"

John frowned, and Derek thought he could see John's left eye vibrate. "I hate to be the bearer of bad news, but I looked in every location that we treated, and apparently we haven't removed any so far. There have not been any reports of them in the glue boards, and no dead bodies anywhere."

"You must be kidding. None at all?"

John was puzzled. He'd expected to find dead, trapped cockroaches. "None. I can't figure out what's going on. There should be at least a few dead ones, if there were roughly fifty that got in yesterday. I'm not sure what to do next."

Derek didn't think it was such a difficult problem. "The other day, you said we'd just up the ante and place more traps and poison. I'm reluctant to have you spray insecticide yet. So, why don't you get started on putting out more traps and poison?"

While John roamed the building seeking out more sites for his glue traps, Derek returned to his desk to catch up on some paperwork. The IT department was being flooded with reports of inoperable or flaky equipment, and the security department was receiving calls from people claiming that someone inside the company was sabotaging its equipment. It was unusual that so many calls had come in literally overnight.

As he scanned the reports, he failed to see a pattern. There were reports of failed desktop and laptop computers, and dysfunctional printers and copiers. Some areas of Wi-Fi coverage were out because the Wi-Fi antennas in the overhead ceiling spaces had stopped working. The IT department reported that inside their data center, at least ten servers, two routers, and five Ethernet switches had failed. It was certainly strange that so many devices had failed in just one night. The reports said that in most cases the equipment was so damaged that replacements would be required.

Hopefully, the insurance would help, but Derek wasn't sure. Paying for it was not his problem, anyway. Figuring out how it happened and who did it was his responsibility.

How could this have happened? Was Julia right that the cockroach prank and this apparent equipment sabotage might be the work of a disgruntled employee? Or maybe several? If so, they would probably still be working here; breaking in from the outside would be difficult. Derek didn't need another problem, like questions about possible negligence involving inadequate security of the building.

Derek decided to inspect the damaged equipment himself; he was hoping to pursue ideas about the methods used and possibly gather clues that would lead him to the perpetrators. He started in the data center—the most severely damaged area.

The data center was located in the center of the building inside a room about fifty feet square with two rows of rack-mounted equipment including servers, routers, Ethernet switches, and all of the connecting cables and power cords. It did not have a raised floor, and the ceiling was open to improve ventilation. The data center hosted all of the company's business applications— accounting, billing, and customer support, as well as applications supporting their engineering department. Access was secured by a badge system, so only authorized personnel were allowed to enter.

Ben Rodham, the IT manager, showed him around the room and pointed out the damaged equipment. Derek was not a computer expert but that didn't mean he couldn't understand what he was seeing. Several of the disabled servers showed weird damage on their intake screens on the front. The metal was sort of melted or corroded, creating a small circular hole in the screen. Ben pulled one of the servers out so they could look inside and showed Derek that here and there various circuit boards and internal components were similarly eaten away or corroded. Ben said the whole server would have to be replaced.

The disabled routers and Ethernet switches had similar damage: holes in the intake vents and internal corrosion. On some of the other equipment, the network cables on the back were melted and broken. Obviously, all the damaged network cables would need to be replaced.

Derek was not an expert, but he thought back to his high school chemistry class and was reminded of what a strong acid could do. So, perhaps some saboteur had managed to inject acid into this equipment.

What a sick asshole, he thought. It also made him think that he should be careful about what he touched in case any acid lingered on the surfaces.

Derek shared his inclinations with Ben, who perked up and said, "That makes sense. I couldn't resist touching things, particularly the odd holes in the vent screens, and almost immediately my skin began to burn. I had to run to the bathroom to wash my hands."

"Yep. That sounds like acid. Let your team know that they need to be careful. Acid contact with the skin can be harmful. And god forbid, you touch your eyes."

"Got it. I'll let them know. Who would do such a thing?" Ben mused.

Derek paused and took a look around the room. "We think it might be some disgruntled employee, but we have no evidence or suspects."

Ben nodded. "Probably right. A lot of people are unhappy about the recent layoffs. Nobody wants to be next."

Derek looked at him sympathetically. "You got that right. I have a big mortgage and three children, and I can't afford to be out of work."

Ben was forced to agree. "I'm in a similar situation. Big mortgage. No kids. Lots of student loan debt."

If they had been more observant, they would have noticed that on the floor below some of the damaged equipment there were small piles of melted light brown, gray, and black debris. Hardly noticeable and impossible to determine what its original shape had been. Inside these globs were small translucent pellets resembling gel pills. Neither Derek nor Ben had any way of knowing that these were clues.

Likewise, neither suspected any connection between the cockroach infestation and the damaged equipment. Why would they? Cockroaches were pests, but hardly capable of causing huge malfunctions like Alligator Enterprises was experiencing.

CHAPTER THREE

Gigabit Western Networking Corporation was an established manufacturer of large-scale Internet routers and Ethernet switches in Sunnyvale, in the heart of Silicon Valley. They had started as a producer of Ethernet switches and over a twenty-five-year period had expanded their product line to become a major name in the communications industry. Recently they had moved to their new campus of fifteen modern two- and three-story buildings of beige stucco with blue metal framed windows and doors. All of the buildings were on the same conjoined plot of land, hence the use of the term "campus" to describe their configuration. Like many of the high-tech companies in Silicon Valley, they had a large gym facility on-site, which included an Olympic-sized swimming pool, as well as three subsidized employee cafeterias. For a brief time, early in the company's history, they had also provided other conveniences, such as pick-up and drop-off of dry cleaning. And for a while, Friday was the employees' favorite day because the company delivered free bagels and cream cheese to the break rooms.

Most outsiders assumed these amenities were provided just because the company had extra money to burn. Just part of the spoiled Silicon Valley culture to pamper the quirky engineers. However, the unspoken reason was to entice employees to stay on campus for longer hours and to be more productive. No time lost driving out for lunch or errands in the middle of the day.

After the financial crisis of 2008–09, many of these perks were scaled back to save money. No more bagels, no more dry-cleaning support, reduced access to the gym, etc. And like most other companies in the area, Gigabit was seeking other ways to cut expenses. Often, that led to painful layoffs and unfortunately, the company had just had a layoff a few months ago. About ten percent of the workforce was "affected"—a euphemism meaning they were released. Some of the lucky ones were offered an early-retirement package, which was quite generous. But that was only the 55 and older crowd with at least ten years of service. The rest only received the minimum of two weeks of pay for each year of service. Gigabit also implemented what they called "self-service reception areas." It was a simple solution. Visitors who entered the lobby were not greeted by a live receptionist. Instead, the signs pointed them to the lobby telephone and invited them to dial the extension of the employee they were there to meet. A PC was conveniently located at the desk, so the visitor could look up the extension. Then, after dialing, they would just wait in the lobby until they were escorted inside by a company employee. It was a pretty straightforward system; workable but not too friendly. In the case of a delivery, the same method was used to notify someone to come to the lobby and pick up packages.

The UPS driver who drove up to Building 12 was familiar with this system, so he rolled his dolly stacked with several boxes into the lobby and called the contact. "Sanjit, this is UPS. There's a box here for you."

"What is it? I wasn't expecting any deliveries."

"I don't know. It's not too big, and it's apparently a computer server. At least that's what the description on the carton says."

"Okay. Thanks. Please just leave it there. I'll come down shortly."

"Sure. Catch you on the back nine." The UPS guy was a bundle of laughs.

Sanjit arrived ten minutes later. He thought it was strange to receive an unexpected computer, but that maybe the lab manager had ordered it as a replacement and had forgotten to tell him. At any rate, he carried it up to the second floor and set it in the corner near some racks of data equipment. He didn't have time to deal with it right at that moment, so he returned to his office to work on some paperwork.

About two hours later, the lab manager, Francisco Ayala, strolled into the lab. He immediately noticed the box in the corner. Since he'd worked at the company for fifteen years and managed all the lab equipment, he was always aware of any changes, and this box certainly had not been there earlier. He took his pen knife from his pants pocket and cut the tape. As soon as he swung the flaps back out of the way, he was startled by a rush of reddish-brown things that looked like insects hurtling out of the box. He jumped back as the insects scrambled in all directions and there seemed to be hundreds of them. He didn't attempt to catch any of them; it would have been futile anyway since they moved so quickly.

He reached his hands up and clutched the top of his head. *What the hell? What's up with this? What kind of sick joke is this? I better let security know. Maybe they can figure out who's responsible.*

Francisco pulled his phone out and called security. "You guys won't believe this, but I just opened a box in the lab and hundreds of insects, or something, came running out all over the place."

Dave Emerson answered in a clearly irritated tone. "Francisco, this isn't funny."

Francisco's voice got louder as he became more annoyed. "Dave, I'm not pranking you. This really happened. What should I do?"

"Where is the box from?"

"It was delivered to the lobby earlier today by UPS. Sanjit brought it up to the lab. I just saw it there and wanted to see what was inside."

Dave couldn't resist asking a leading question. "Why'd you open it if it was filled with insects?"

Francisco replied testily, "That's a ridiculous question! I didn't know what was inside. The box was labeled as a computer server. It seemed legitimate."

"What kind of insects are they? How many came out of the box?"

Francisco calmed down. "I'm not sure, but I think cockroaches. They were moving so fast and I didn't get a real good look, but that's what they looked like. I have no idea how many. I guess we're talking about several hundred."

"And where are they now?"

Francisco's frustration was renewed. "Another ridiculous question. Where do you *think* they are? They've scattered all over the lab. They're everywhere—probably hiding in nooks and crannies."

Dave decided to back off a bit. "Okay. No need to be sarcastic. I was just asking. You have to admit that this is bizarre."

"You're right about that."

"I'll call maintenance and report it so they can get on top of exterminating them."

"Thanks." Francisco was relieved to move the problem off his plate. It wasn't in his job description to take care of cockroach infestations.

After Dave hung up, he placed a call to the maintenance department. After he heard the laughter die down in the background, they agreed to help. Both Dave and the maintenance supervisor were well aware that if in fact these were cockroaches, it was important to get rid of them quickly before they could establish a colony.

Dave turned back to his desk, and in the short time he'd been on the phone he'd received two voicemails. They were describing the exact same problem to him that was originating in two other buildings on the campus. *That's strange*, he thought. Unfortunately for Dave, his troubles were just beginning. By the end of the day, identical incidents had been reported in seven more labs, bringing the total to ten infested labs in ten different buildings. This would be a nightmare for pest control.

Dave didn't believe that it was a coincidence. Someone was creating this nuisance—probably a disgruntled employee. Maybe several. The first priority would be to deal with the infestations and then later he would have time to search for perpetrators.

CHAPTER FOUR

The labs at Gigabit Western Networking Corporation were used to develop new products, testing and validating them as they moved from concepts to alpha and beta testing to public release. Some engineers were involved in proof-of-concept testing to support sales teams. And in one of the labs, the engineers were focused on testing products from competitors in order to discover vulnerabilities that the sales force could use in competitive sales situations.

A typical lab contained rows of lab benches set apart by aisles. These rows extended for one to two hundred feet, often across the width of the building. The lab benches were interspersed with standardized vertical racks to mount computer servers, Ethernet switches, routers, or test equipment. The front of the equipment usually faced the aisle, and on the reverse side, the racks were positioned so that the rear was back-to-back with the adjacent aisle. Typically, all of the cables and power cords were located on this rear side, but that wasn't universally the case. Power outlets were in ceiling racks and much of the interconnecting cabling also ran vertically from the equipment up to the ceiling. It might look chaotic, but it was in fact quite organized and efficient.

And it represented a wealth of targets for a saboteur, and there had been an orgy of destruction that night.

The next morning, strange reports started flooding into the security department. Engineering teams throughout the campus were calling to report damage in their labs. Reports described holes eaten into the intake vents of servers, routers, and Ethernet switches, often accompanied by internal damage. Other reports concerned connecting cables and power cords that were corroded and eaten through. The damage had occurred in ten of the labs on campus. In total, Dave had been given a rough count of 200 servers, 37 routers, and 17 Ethernet switches that were knocked out of operation. Not to mention innumerable network cables and power cords and miscellaneous units of smaller equipment. It was a disaster.

How is this possible? Dave thought. The descriptions of the damage indicated that it could have only been caused by someone with physical access. That is, they must have been in the building. So, either they were current employees or former employees who had been given access by an insider or broken in. Also, it must have involved more than one perpetrator since it had occurred in ten different buildings.

Dave was stumped. *This week has rapidly turned into shit. First that cockroach prank. And now a serious saboteur on the loose. What's next? Too bad I wasn't offered that early retirement package a few months ago.*

First he needed to get together with the exterminators to fix the insect issue. Then he'd have to address the sabotage problem. That would involve contacting the authorities because clearly there were criminals at work here. He had no reason to think that the two situations were connected. After all, a cockroach problem was serious, but nobody ever heard of them destroying equipment. It was unimaginable to Dave.

So far nobody had noticed the small globs on the floor near the damaged areas.

CHAPTER FIVE

When he was contacted about the cockroach problem at Gigabit, Richard Cheney, the owner of BugsBGone Pest Management, dispatched two technicians to the campus. Clearly this was a major infestation, and he wanted to ensure that he allocated the appropriate resources to this valued customer. Armando Figueroa and Luis Chavez had both worked at BugsBGone for at least ten years. Between the two of them, they'd managed hundreds of cockroach infestations. Both Armando and Luis planned to use the standard approach, though on a much larger scale.

Meeting in the conference room beforehand, Armando filled in Dave and Phil. "The first thing we need to do is map out where they're concentrated. Then we can place liquid gel and bait traps in the right areas. We'll install roach motels behind equipment, near crevasses or cracks, and under sinks. Basically, anywhere that they're likely to hide or look for food. Once we see where we're trapping them, we can focus on next steps—putting out poison bait or boric acid, which is probably the most effective long-term poison, but we don't want to just scatter it everywhere at the beginning; that's not efficient."

"Okay," Dave figured. "That makes sense, I guess. You two are the experts, not me. But why don't we just spray insecticide instead?"

Armando turned in his chair and briefly glanced over at Luis as if he needed some silent approval for what he was about to say. "We don't like to spray insecticides unless absolutely necessary. People don't like it in their environment, so it's generally a last resort. Besides, we can't spray until we know *where* they are."

Dave shrugged. "Fine. I understand. So when can you get started?"

"Right away. Luis and I will divide up the buildings. We need access stat."

Dave nodded. "Certainly. I'll get you temporary badges, so you won't have to be shadowed by a security person." Dave made a call to his security department asking them to bring two temporary employee badges to the conference room.

Armando smiled, thinking that it would be really nice not to have a security person babysitting him everywhere he went. "Great. We'll start bringing the glue traps in from our truck. We should have plenty, but our office is close in case we need more." After staring up at the ceiling briefly lost in thought, Armando added, "One more thing: would you send out a notification telling personnel not to discard the traps or pick up any dead cockroaches? I know they'd probably like to clean up, but we'd like to see evidence ourselves. We'll be back in two days to do that, and I promise we'll clean up the cockroaches ourselves."

Dave nodded, but he was thinking, *I'm pretty sure people would rather not have a bunch of cockroach carcasses lying around.* But he replied, "You got it. I'll send out a company-wide memo today. Is there anything else you need?"

Armando considered this question for a moment and then said, "Not right now. I'll let you know. Luis, let's get started."

CHAPTER SIX

Armando and Luis returned to Gigabit two days later. After scouring the buildings for about six hours, they returned to Dave's office to give him a report. Phil came in to join them.

"Dave, we told you not to clean," Armando started. "We've inspected all of the areas where we placed the traps. We didn't find a single cockroach. Nor did we find any dead ones. And curiously, we didn't see any of the other typical signs such as small brown fecal pellets anywhere."

Dave looked over at Phil for a moment then turned back to Armando with a sort of blank expression. "That doesn't make sense—no one picked up the carcasses. You can see the traps are still there, aren't they?"

Armando shook his head back and forth to emphasize his confusion. "Then we've never seen anything like this. You're saying they just disappeared into thin air? Are you sure there really were cockroaches in the first place? Were the reports just made up?"

Dave became annoyed. "That would mean engineers in ten buildings conspired on a prank on me. That would be pretty farfetched—most of them are too busy to be bothered with stupid jokes."

Armando was a bit irritated himself, because he felt like his expertise was being questioned. "If you say so. I'm telling you that so far, we can't locate any evidence that the cockroaches were here. We seem to be dealing with imaginary cockroaches, so what do you want us to do?"

Dave let the sarcastic comment land without a direct response. "I'm not sure. I suppose all you can do is watch the traps for a few more days, and then if there's still nothing, we'll call off the hunt." Out of the corner of his eye, he could see Phil shrugging as if to indicate that the answer was pretty obvious.

Armando and Luis returned to their office at BugsBGone. They updated their boss on the situation, and he was just as puzzled as the two technicians. It just didn't make sense. But his mind was elsewhere.

"While you're waiting on the Gigabit problem, I need you to work on a few other projects. I've received calls from three more companies in similar situations. Each reported cockroach deliveries in shipping boxes, and the bugs are loose in their buildings. I don't know what's going on. It's the weirdest thing I've heard of. Get started on these new projects right away but keep a close eye on Gigabit."

CHAPTER SEVEN

INTERLUDE: THE COVID-19 PANDEMIC BEGINS IN CALIFORNIA

THE FIRST CASE OF COVID-19 IN CALIFORNIA was confirmed by the CDC on January 25, 2020, in an individual who'd recently traveled to Wuhan, China. The second case was revealed on January 31 in another individual who'd recently traveled to Wuhan. On January 29, the U.S. State Department evacuated 195 of its employees, their families, and other citizens from Hubei Province to be quarantined at a U.S. military base. Subsequently, another 345 citizens were evacuated from China to be quarantined at two military air bases in California: Travis Air Force Base in Solano County and Marine Corps Air Station Miramar in San Diego. Another group of evacuees was brought home on February 6 and placed into quarantine at military bases in Nebraska and Texas.

Shortly after that, the government brought home 338 nationals stranded in Yokohama, Japan, on the cruise ship *Diamond Princess*. They were quarantined at Travis Air Force Base near Sacramento. At least fourteen of these individuals tested positive for the virus.

On February 26, the first case of "community transmission"—that is, person-to-person spread—was identified in the U.S., a case with no known origin, discovered in Solano County. After that, the COVID-19 virus spread rapidly throughout the state of California. The spread was uneven, with the major infection centers in the more populous counties.

COVID-19 was just starting to spread widely at about the same time as the attacks at Alligator Enterprises occurred.

The pattern in any pandemic is that the spread of an infectious disease has an exponential growth curve. In simple terms, this means that even though early numbers seem small, they can quickly rise. For example, if each person infects two others, those two become four, four become eight, eight become sixteen, and so forth. It can rapidly escalate. In California, this pattern was clear in the actual numbers of cases. On January 26, there were two cases; on February 6, six cases; and by March 5, 60 cases; March 15, 472 cases; and March 20, 1,224 cases. This increase occurred in a six-week period. And it continued to grow. As of March 28, the total had reached 4,702. Exponential growth is rapid and relentless. As of December 1, 2020, there were over 1.2 million cases in California.

Around the United States, certain areas had become early hot beds, most notably New York City, Washington state, and California, with other areas like Florida, Arizona, and Louisiana also turning into hot spots.

A state of emergency was put in place in the State of California on March 4, 2020. On March 19, Governor Gavin Newsom announced a mandatory stay-at-home order for the entire state. Only essential businesses, such as gas stations, grocery stores, banks, pharmacies, auto repair shops, and dry cleaners could remain open. Bars, restaurants, schools, and even wineries were shut down. The financial impact from these closures was enormous. For example, in just the first two months of the crisis, over 35 million people became unemployed, air travel dropped about 95 percent, and hotel bookings plummeted. Restaurants were forced to change their business model to takeout only. It was estimated that as many as 30 percent of them would never reopen.

There were other consequences of the shutdown. A large percentage of the work force was forced to work from home, and parents also had to be responsible for day care and home-schooling.

Social distancing rules were implemented as well as the recommendation, and later requirement, to wear a medical mask in public to reduce the risk of spreading the virus as much as possible. These measures were met with mixed reactions, to say the least, and became political flashpoints, an unfortunate development. After all, the COVID-19 virus had no political agenda, its only agenda (if you could call it that) was to spread as widely as possible. The entire economy went into a tailspin as unemployment skyrocketed and the economy headed for recession. Health experts agreed that this was the only way to prevent the pandemic from totally overwhelming the healthcare system; the United States simply didn't have the hospital capacity or medical staffing to handle the numbers of expected cases.

How is this related to the investigations of sabotage at Silicon Valley companies? The spread of COVID-19 throughout California, and the steps taken to slow it down would have unprecedented consequences for the local FBI on the case. It would cause disruptions and unforeseen problems for their investigations of the data center attacks.

PART II

CHAPTER EIGHT

FEBRUARY 2020

Things had been pretty quiet for FBI Special Agent Maxwell Smart in the Oakland office. It had been about a year since his team cracked the case of the nefarious Chinese toy robot fire attacks, Project Inferno. In part, things had quieted down because it had been solved and halted. The Chinese had continued to deny any involvement. And no one was interested in causing panic. Of course, that didn't stop the tin foil hat crowd from spinning conspiracy theories, but there wasn't really anything to be done about that. Those nut rolls would always find something to slant or fabricate when necessary. Ultimately, Max was relieved because the case had been convoluted and stressful, and he was happy to have it in his rearview mirror.

He sat at his desk gazing pensively out the window of his tenth-floor office at the high-rise buildings across the Bay. To the left side of his view was the graceful arc of the rebuilt Bay Bridge connecting Oakland to downtown San Francisco. In the far distance, he could see the orange Golden Gate bridge shrouded in a fog bank. And all across the Bay, there were numerous large and small boats moving about from large lumbering freighters to graceful sailboats. He never tired of this view.

It was another sunny and warm day in the Bay Area, and he resented being stuck in the office with endless paperwork. What he really desired was to be outdoors. For Max, it felt like retirement could not happen too soon. He was in his late forties, so he had several more years before he would be forced to take mandatory retirement, so he had to put these thoughts out of his mind for now.

He was tall and lanky, though it was probably just because of good genetics; it certainly wasn't the result of working out. He had dark brown hair which fortunately in his opinion had not started to gray. That would come in time, he was sure. All he had to do was look at his aging father to be reminded of what was coming. Probably because of the stress of his twenty-plus years with the FBI, his face always seemed to convey a worried look. But he was an excellent investigator and well-liked by his colleagues.

Max was startled from his daydreaming by the loud ringing of his desk phone. He glanced at the color display to see it was his supervisor, Thomas Fitzgerald. He couldn't just ignore it. Calls from the boss must always be answered, especially since Tom was down the hall and probably fully aware that Max was there.

"Hey, Tom, what's up?"

"Please come to my office. I have a new case I need you to get started on."

"I'll be right there."

Just what he needed. More work. Max entered Tom's office a few minutes later, moving gingerly.

"Your back still bothering you?" Tom asked.

Max couldn't help wincing as he sat down. "Yes. Most of the doctors say I'll just have to tolerate the pain for the rest of my life. They don't think they can fix the underlying problem, though I'm scheduled to have exploratory surgery in May. I'm working with a new back specialist at Stanford Hospital. He thinks he may have a solution."

"Can't you take more painkillers?" Tom asked.

Max shook his head and sighed. "I don't want to. Besides, you need your best agent to be alert, right? Opioids might prevent me from thinking clearly."

"I suppose that'd be a problem if I had any good agents who needed to be clear-headed. But I'm stuck with you," Tom replied with a wry smile.

Max and Tom had worked together for about ten years and this banter was par for the course. Truthfully, Tom did think Max was an outstanding agent and had often counted on him in the past. He figured he would be the perfect agent for this new case.

Tom explained his dilemma. "But seriously, Max, we've been receiving numerous reports of widespread damage to equipment within companies. So far it's focused on the Silicon Valley, but they are starting to spread further north."

"What type of damage are we talking about?" Max asked as he pulled out a small notebook and started jotting down notes.

"Well, the reports are strange," Tom continued. "Some of the companies report that in labs or computer centers, up to half of the equipment is knocked out in a single night. In many cases, the computers and other equipment are damaged beyond repair, so they must be replaced. As you can imagine, the costs add up fast, and the owners are totally pissed off about it."

Max looked up from his notebook. "What type of damage, specifically?"

Tom looked out the window as he contemplated his answer. "In many of the reports they use the term *corrosion* and mention *melted parts*. I don't know exactly what that means. They say it could be intentional. It doesn't seem likely that damage would occur overnight to numerous computers unless it was sabotage. Most of these companies believe that it was probably caused by employees who have been recently laid off and are still angry."

Max took his turn gazing out the window. "That could be a logical assumption."

Tom added, "Some of the attacks were in open, public areas. But some occurred in highly secure areas, which implicates current employees, or someone working with them."

Max thought that also was a logical conclusion. "What do you want me to do?"

Tom had already thought about a plan. "I've sent you the reports. Please start interviewing the companies. This is getting out of hand. Right now, there are over thirty companies who have been victimized, and it seems that the list is growing rapidly. We may have an organized criminal network at work, so we need to solve this case as fast as we can. As you can imagine, the longer it goes unresolved, the more heat we'll take. And God forbid something leaks to the press, the heat will be unbelievable. I think the only reason it hasn't made the news yet is that the companies are too embarrassed to talk about it."

Max shook his head as if he was clearing it out. "Tom, this obviously costs the victimized companies a lot of money. Setting aside the idea of disgruntled employees, is it possible that this is some elaborate extortion scheme?"

Tom hesitated. "Sure, I suppose. But none of the reports have mentioned demands for money, or any motives. Perhaps the perps are just setting the stage for later. I don't have a clue."

"Sounds like our first approach is to look for angry current or former employees."

"I agree. Let me know as soon as you discover anything."

Max couldn't resist a slight dig and replied with a smile. "Will do. Thanks for the assignment. I didn't have enough on my plate already. By the way, this could become a pretty large case. Can I ask other agents to get involved?"

Tom waved a hand as if to dismiss him. "No problem. You're the right guy for the job, and I trust your judgement. Recruit anyone you need."

Max headed back to his office to start reviewing the reports. In spite of his complaining, he actually enjoyed working on interesting cases. And this case certainly promised to be quite interesting. His first impression was that the stack of reports was pretty overwhelming. He wasn't sure where to start. He thought about sorting them—by the date they were filed, or location—but he decided to just bite the bullet and read through them in the order they were stacked on his desk. His plan was to look for patterns, such as methods or tools that might have been used. With so many companies reporting damages, he also wanted to narrow the list down to a subset of the best candidates to interview. This process took up the remainder of his day. And each time he looked out the window, he was reminded that he'd rather be on one of those beautiful sailboats out on the bay.

In order to kick-start his investigation, he narrowed the list to two companies: a small one called Alligator Enterprises, located in Mountain View and a larger one called Gigabit Western Networking Corporation in Sunnyvale. The two cities actually abutted each other, which would make visiting them convenient. He grabbed his phone and set up interviews with representatives from each one. Next, he thought about who he should add to his team and immediately two local agents came to mind: Jason Forster and Monica Selden. They'd worked with him previously, and he had always been pleased with their contributions. So, he contacted each of them and asked them to join him for coffee in the cafeteria where he hoped a free cup of coffee, and maybe a treat, would entice them to join the team.

When the three met in the cafeteria about an hour later, he ushered them to a distant corner. Both of them noticed this and quickly glanced at each other, but neither commented on it.

"I'd like you two to join my team to work on a large case that just came in. For now, we need to treat this information as highly confidential. To cut to the chase, someone is running around the Bay Area destroying equipment at tech companies. We don't know yet, but it appears to be sabotage by someone either currently or formerly associated with these companies."

Monica spoke up first. "How do you know it's an affiliate of the companies?"

"As I said, we don't know that for a fact, but it's the working premise. Also, it gives us a logical place to start gathering clues."

Jason leaned forward. "What do you need from us?"

"Well, the case will involve a lot of old-fashioned legwork from all of us. There are reports from thirty companies on my desk. I propose that we divide them up and start the work contacting each company for suspects. I can't think of another approach, at least not at the beginning."

"So, you're talking about ten companies each? That'll be a lot of interviews," Monica noted.

"I know, but it can't be avoided," Max agreed. "We need to get moving as fast as we can. If it gets any publicity, the heat will really be on us to solve it. And, as you know, many of these companies are politically connected. I assume we all want to avoid that heat if possible."

"You're absolutely right. The work is hard enough; we don't need politicians breathing down our necks," Monica added with a hint of sarcasm.

Max thought that her comment was painfully obvious so he didn't respond, just changed the subject. "Okay. Let's go back to my office, and I'll give you each ten folders describing the incidents. I suggest that you figure out the best ones to start with. It may not be necessary to interview all ten, there's always the chance that a pattern will emerge early allowing us to narrow down the list of suspects. I'm not promising that by any means, but we can always hope for a lucky break."

When he returned to his office, Max handed them their individual stacks of files. When Jason received his stack, he motioned to Max that he wanted to speak with him. Monica left because it was clear from his posture and furtive look that Jason wanted some privacy.

Jason seemed uncomfortable and avoided looking Max directly in the eye. "I would like a favor," he said. "I just helped my parents move into an assisted living facility in Santa Clara, and I would like to take off for a couple days to make sure they're settled in. It's a big move for them because they had lived in their house in Santa Clara for forty years. As you know, that's where I grew up."

Max didn't think the time off would be a problem. "I understand. My parents are facing that tough decision as well, though I think they'll probably wait a few more years. These sabotage cases are pretty high priority. Do you think you could do some of the initial legwork by phone over the next few days while you're with your folks?"

41

"Yes. I shouldn't need more than a day or two. I appreciate your flexibility."

"No worries. Keep me in the loop if anything changes."

"I will. Thanks."

CHAPTER NINE

Max left Oakland around ten the next morning and drove south down the 880 freeway, connected with Highway 237, and arrived at Alligator Enterprises in Mountain View about an hour later. In this neighborhood, all of the businesses were single-story tilt-up construction, tidy and professional-looking, though unremarkable. Certainly not flashy by any measure. Max thought the company name was silly, but no crazier than others in Silicon Valley. The logo on the front of the building seemed corny to him.

The one trend that he really couldn't tolerate was when internet companies started their names with a lowercase letter. That was a trend he could really do without. At least Alligator Enterprises hadn't adopted that silly marketing trick.

Julia Tucker met Max in the lobby, and after he introduced himself as Agent Smart, he also introduced the two local FBI forensic investigators, Jonathon Thompson and Andrew Hutchinson who'd met him on-site. Julia nodded politely and motioned for them to follow her down the hall. She escorted them to a meeting room in the center of the building where they were met by Derek Jonason, the security director, and Ben Rodham, the IT manager.

Derek introduced himself and Ben. "Agent Smart, we really appreciate you jumping on this case so quickly."

"That's my job, and I'm happy to help. Derek, as I understand it, you filed the report about the incident, right?"

"That's correct."

"I've read the report, but please describe the incident for me in your own words."

"Okay. It's actually pretty simple. Ben came into my office and told me that overnight much of the equipment in our data center had unexpectedly failed. Many of the servers, routers, and Ethernet switches were out of service. Some were completely dead, while others were operating but had flashing error lights indicating internal failures. Outside the data center, a few printers and fax machines had stopped working as well. And, in a few cases, workers' computers in the office areas were damaged. It all happened that same night."

Jonathon spoke up. "What specific kind of damage did you observe?"

"That was the strange part," said Derek. "Often the damage seemed trivial. For example, many of the failed devices had small corroded holes in their intake vents. Also, we opened some of the failed equipment and found internal areas, such as circuit boards or wiring, that had corroded."

Jonathon nodded. "What do you think caused it?"

"I don't know. Obviously, they had been exposed to some sort of corrosive material."

"Clearly that's the case. But what specifically would corrode these things?"

Derek had a quick response. "Well, my best guess would be some sort of strong acid."

Max though about that for a minute: "How do you think it got into the equipment?"

Ben couldn't hold back any longer, so he finally spoke up. "It doesn't take much imagination to figure that out. Someone had to have physical access to the equipment so they could somehow inject acid directly into the vent or chassis. They would have to be inside the data center."

Max turned to Ben. "Is that why you wrote in your incident report that it was done by a disgruntled employee?"

Ben looked as if the answer should be obvious. "Sure seems logical to us."

"But don't you restrict access to the data center?" Max asked.

Since this was a security matter, Derek interjected. "Well, the office areas are less secure, but yes, you need a valid badge to enter the data center. Only a few current employees would have badges."

"But wouldn't that be a pretty stupid move?" asked Max. "I assume you have records showing who used their badges and when? That would reveal their identity right away. Right?"

Derek was nonplussed. "Of course, but you're assuming they're thinking about the consequences of their actions. Maybe they were so angry that they threw caution to the wind."

"I guess that's possible," Max conceded. "But I don't think it's likely. I've been chasing criminals for a long time, and my experience is that they always try to hide the evidence." After he let that sink in, he asked another question. "Tell me about former employees. Could they have an access badge?"

Derek shook his head. "That's a remote possibility, but unlikely. When an employee leaves the company for any reason, we make them turn in their badge to human resources. That's a standard part of the exit interview. And we track the badges carefully. A former employee couldn't keep their badge—if they did, it would be inactivated."

"Could they steal one from a current employee?"

"I suppose, but like I said, we'd know because we track them carefully."

"I would like to focus on the disgruntled employee possibility," Max asserted. "This is a loaded question, but are there any likely candidates that come to mind? Anyone you know personally who might hold a grudge?"

"Well, none come to mind immediately, but we've had some recent layoffs. Some of those people could be candidates."

"Who can provide me with that list?"

"HR can."

"You mentioned that people who are released have an exit interview. What happens at that exit interview?"

Derek had been through the process recently when he had to lay off a person from his department, so he was pretty familiar with it. "Well, as I mentioned, they turn in their access badge and any company property, such as phones or laptops. Usually, they're provided with an exit package including compensation, COBRA coverage, and some pointers to assist them in finding another job. They must sign a waiver promising they won't sue for any reason. If they refuse to sign, they don't get a severance check. They're asked if they want to provide any feedback, positive or negative, to the HR representative."

Max's interest was piqued. "I'm intrigued. What do people typically say?"

Derek glanced at Ben. "I haven't done many exit interviews myself, but I've heard that most people choose not to say anything. Positive comments come from younger employees who share their thanks for the opportunity. Negative comments come from people who are angry to be out of a job and assume that they were singled out for elimination for some awful reason. Might be that their boss hated them. Might be gender or age discrimination. That's probably the most common negative feedback—age bias."

Max thought about this and concluded that it might provide some valuable leads. "So, if the person expressed anger, I assume HR would keep notes on that?"

"Of course," Derek responded sarcastically, "they probably also keep notes about people's attitudes or body language, which I assume would also give valuable clues."

Max looked calmly at Derek. "I think you're correct. I'd like to see a list of employees who were terminated in your last layoff. Later we can look further back if necessary."

Surprisingly, HR provided him a short list. Two employees had departed angrily: David Johnson and William Kane. He would track them down and interview them.

Alligator Enterprises had a small security operations center that was managed by Derek. It was located in the administrative area and housed several computers and ten monitors connected to the surveillance cameras, some of which covered the front, back, and sides of the building. The computers logged events like badge access on all the doors, even the ones in the shipping docks. These were monitored by Derek's small staff, and all video feeds were saved on the system. Derek went back to his office to look for any video evidence of intrusions. He wanted to make sure he hadn't missed anything.

The two FBI forensic investigators, Jonathon and Andrew, were escorted to the computer room to gather evidence. Upon entering, they both noticed an acrid and faintly irritating odor, but neither of them could identify it. However, it was slightly painful to breathe, and their eyes watered. They asked Ben if he could open some doors and turn up the fans to clear out the air.

The team proceeded to dust equipment for fingerprints, not really expecting to find anything important, but the process was pro forma. They asked Ben if they could remove some items, like a few of the damaged servers, and if he would permit them to send these to the FBI lab for chemical analysis. Of course, he agreed.

They also noticed the small brownish globs on the floor here and there that seemed to be melted, and they saw small, oval-shaped objects in the debris. They collected several of these and forwarded them to the FBI lab along with the damaged equipment. Neither of them had any clue what the blobs were, but since they were scattered in the crime scene, they assumed that they might be significant.

CHAPTER TEN

Milton Fry was a technician in the FBI laboratory in Quantico, Virginia, on the scientific/chemistry team. He had worked there for about ten years and was an experienced technician who had extensive training as a chemist. Earlier that day, Milton had received the various pieces of equipment and envelopes of evidence from the forensics team in California. He set the servers, routers, and Ethernet switches on the lab tables and placed the clear evidence bags containing odd brownish globs of debris off to the side. He planned to start by examining the damage, then focus on chemical analysis of the weird-looking globs. He used a digital camera to document what he saw.

A quick examination of one of the servers did not reveal much physical damage, with the exception of a small corroded area on the front air vents. He glanced at the other devices and saw similar damage, although sometimes there were two or more corroded holes in the vents.

Milton took the top off one of the servers. Again, there wasn't a lot of visible internal damage. However, a closer examination of some of the circuit boards showed surface corrosion that had eaten into the delicate circuitry. There was also corrosion on the hard drives, fans, and power supplies. He assumed that the server had failed largely because of the damage to the circuit boards. Also, some of the internal wiring had eroded, disconnecting some components. Milton was not a computer expert, but it didn't take a geek to see that this server had been knocked out of operation by damage to key internal components.

Milton opened the other two servers and the two routers and one Ethernet switch he had received and found similar damage to critical internal components in all of them. It was not always the same area. For example, in one server, it was the main circuit board which had knocked out the CPU. In another, it was the circuit board on the hard drive, the circuit board responsible for controlling the hard drive itself. So, the damage was sort of random, or at least not targeted to any particular components.

While working on his overview of the damage, he had noticed a pungent odor, slightly irritating to his eyes and throat. It was consistent with the presence of an acid, so he felt better about pursuing that angle.

Based on his survey of the damage, he came to two conclusions: first, the damage appeared to have been caused by some strong acid, and second, it looked like someone had squirted it into the equipment through the front vents. So, his next step would be to identify the specific acid used. How it was injected was not as important.

The lab was equipped with portable gas detectors capable of detecting a variety of exotic gases, such as hydrogen bromide, hydrogen chloride, nitric acid, hydrogen peroxide, hydrazine, and hydrogen fluoride. He used the detector probes to identify which gas was emitting the noxious odor. He tried a variety of detectors because each could only detect a single type of gas, but he was finally able to determine that the gas was the extremely poisonous hydrogen fluoride. With that in mind, he realized he would have to be more careful. His detector was reporting less than one part per million, but at levels as low as three to six parts per million, hydrogen fluoride could irritate the lining of the lungs. At levels of ten to fifteen parts per million, exposure would cause irritation to the eyes and skin. At levels between fifty and 250 parts per million, hydrogen fluoride was lethal within minutes.

Milton put on a safety mask. So, what type of acid would emit gaseous hydrogen fluoride? There was only one acid that he knew that fit that criteria, fluoroantimonic acid. It was a so-called "super-acid" notorious for its ability to dissolve just about anything—metals, plastic, glass, and flesh. Definitely dangerous, and it certainly explained the damage he had seen in the equipment.

He turned his attention to the evidence bags with the small brownish globs. In addition to wearing the protective mask, he moved to work under one of the ventilated hoods. He put on gloves and pulled out some stainless-steel forceps to handle the specimens. He opened one of the evidence bags, which curiously had dissolved inside from contact with the specimens, and he immediately noticed the same noxious odor. Apparently, whatever these globs had originally been, they had also been dissolved by the acid. There were about ten specimens in the bag, and they all looked different. There was no way to tell what they had originally been. The only way to describe them was that they had "melted." He resolved to analyze them to see what kinds of compounds they contained. That would take a few days of chemical analysis with sophisticated tools like liquid gas chromatographs or mass spectrometers.

After two days of thorough chemical analysis, Milton determined that the blobs contained a variety of compounds, including a large quantity of low-density polystyrene, lesser quantities of several other types of plastic and ceramic material, and traces of lithium, copper, silicon, boron, graphite, and gold.

Several had hollow, translucent objects in them that resembled oval pills. He couldn't be sure, but his guess was that these had acted as containers for the acid. If so, when analyzed, they would turn out to be Teflon because that was the only substance that could withstand fluoroantimonic acid. And that turned out to be the case once he finished his analysis. So, he had isolated the type of acid that was used, but he still didn't know how the acid got injected into the equipment. But it was time to let the field teams know right away. For several reasons. Of course, they needed to be informed about how the attacks had damaged the equipment. But, most urgently, they needed to be warned about the highly dangerous acid.

CHAPTER ELEVEN

After wrapping up at Alligator Enterprises, Max visited the headquarters of Gigabit. It was a much larger company, fifteen modern buildings spread out over a spacious campus. He drove to Building One, the only three-story building on the company's campus. He parked in the visitors' lot and entered through large stainless steel and glass doors directly into an elegant lobby with a sitting area for guests and a long wooden and metal desk toward the back wall. The receptionist greeted him with a warm smile—this was the only building on campus that had a real person in the lobby.

Max identified himself and asked to see the security director, Dave Emerson. The receptionist placed a quick call, and Dave appeared in the lobby and escorted Max to a small modestly appointed meeting room. Max noticed that this was an unsecured area, and understood that Gigabit took security seriously and used this setup to keep visitors out of secure areas.

Max asked if anyone else should be included.

"I'll call a couple of the lab managers and have them join us." About ten minutes later, Sanjit Gupta and Francisco Ayala strolled into the conference room.

After introductions, Max led the interrogation. "My job is track down whoever perpetrated this crime. We always look for motive, as well as opportunity. As I understand it, the damage was extensive, and it destroyed a lot of costly equipment—all in one night. So instead of talking about the specific damage, I would like you to tell me what *you* think happened."

"Well," Dave responded, "it seems obvious that the person who did this had lab access. Almost all of the damage we saw would require someone to have physical access to the equipment. Our opinion is that this was a sabotage by a former employee."

Max nodded. "Any idea who that might be?"

Dave glanced at Sanjit and Francisco as if inviting their input. "I have a couple candidates in mind. No proof, though."

"Why are these people suspects, in your opinion?" Max asked as he pulled out his notebook to jot down the names.

Dave had apparently thought about this question at length. "Well, one guy, Alfred McCandless, was fired for striking a coworker. He was escorted out of his building immediately by three of my security staff. He was quite animated on his way out, shouting obscenities and threats."

Max turned to make more notes in his notebook. "When was that?"

"About two months ago."

"And you think he'd still be angry enough to retaliate?"

"Who knows? You never know what's going on in someone's head."

Max smiled. "That's for sure. As you can imagine, in my line of work, we spend a lot of time trying to figure out what people are thinking. What about the second suspected former employee you mentioned?"

"He actually worked for Sanjit in one of our labs. His name's Richard Parker. He was responsible for purchasing new lab gear on behalf of the engineers. He took their requests, ordered the items, tracked and received them in the lab, distributed them to the engineers, and kept inventory. Unfortunately, he had cut a deal to siphon off some of these items for an accomplice to sell on the black market. He seemed to believe that Gigabit was so big that the missing gear wouldn't be noticed. What he hadn't counted on was that the ordering system tracked each item by serial number. One day, a customer called in to register a router to start their warranty. The bean counters discovered that the serial number for that router should have been in the lab, not at an actual customer site. Of course, at that point the scheme unraveled. His accomplice was arrested, he was fired, and I think he is currently being prosecuted for felony grand theft. It wouldn't surprise me if he harbored a lot of resentment."

Max looked up after he completed his notes. "Was that recent?"

"About four months ago."

"Okay. I've noted those two names. I'll interview them." Max changed the subject. "I saw in the news that you had some layoffs. Could your HR people provide me some insight into any other employees that departed under less-than-friendly terms?"

"I'm sure they can."

"Great." Max wanted to explore the security angle more. "A couple more questions. Clearly, you take security seriously. Since the attacks on your equipment required physical access, how'd they get inside?"

Dave simply replied, "We don't know. Our badge-tracking system did not show any unauthorized attempts. None of the people who entered or left the labs that night were unauthorized."

"It could have been a current employee, right?" Max asked.

Dave looked over at Sanjit and Francisco as if seeking confirmation. "I don't think so. Since they would show up in the badge access log, that would be a stupid move. Besides, that person would have to have entered ten different labs that night, showing up ten times in the log." He paused. "And one other problem. Two of the labs have so much top-secret information that only a few people are actually allowed inside. That would even further narrow the list. That would be a pretty risky move and just downright stupid."

"What about an individual, or a team of criminals, with stolen credentials?"

Dave just shook his head. "I doubt it, for the same reasons."

Max seemed satisfied. "Just asking to be thorough. I'll start with the two names you just provided, Alfred McCandless and Richard Parker."

CHAPTER TWELVE

O n the way back to his office in Oakland, Max had a long stretch in the car driving up the 880 freeway to reflect on what he'd learned. There was no doubt that the "disgruntled employee" angle was probably the best idea, and he'd start contacting some of the key names.

But the thing that kept bothering him was the sheer volume of incidents. Was it possible that thirty companies had been simultaneously attacked by disgruntled employees? Companies in the Bay Area had plenty of layoffs over the years—it was common in these competitive and high-flying industries. But the layoffs were not connected in any way. These companies didn't conspire to create a whole bunch of disgruntled employees at the same time. That made no sense to him.

Perhaps it was a criminal gang, some unknown collection of collaborators. The problem with that theory was that it would have required many resources to attack dozens of companies, each at its own location. It was possible that the criminal gang had identified the disgruntled employees on their own and used them as collaborators, but that would have required substantial effort.

Besides, what would be the motive for attacking thirty different companies? Max hadn't noticed any commonalities, except for the types and extent of damage. So why would a criminal group be targeting them? So far, no demands had come in for ransom or bribes. Of course, the demands might come in later, so that was still a possibility. But that idea was shelved until it became a reality.

"Connie, I need your help," Max said on the phone to his assistant. He asked her to look up the contact information for all of the names that had been mentioned by both Alligator and Gigabit.

"I'll get started right away."

"Thanks. I'll see you in about an hour." He looked out the windshield at the cars moving with him at about 25 miles per hour.

When he got back to the office, Connie had found information for all four of the suspects he had asked for. Three of them were still living in the Bay Area, but Richard Parker had moved to Poipu on Kauai. If he could prove he was out of state when the attacks happened, he would be off the hook. Max called the three local suspects and set up interviews for the following day.

CHAPTER THIRTEEN

The first suspect Max interviewed was David Johnson, formerly of Alligator Enterprises, and currently living in Santa Clara. He agreed to meet Max at his apartment. David answered the door with a defensive attitude and posture. He was wearing a black t-shirt with a Grateful Dead design, beat-up jeans, and a pair of well-worn flipflops. He appeared to Max to be about fifty years old, but it was hard to pin down his age, since he still had plenty of hair, no premature balding, and it was not graying yet.

"Agent Smart, I need to see your identification before I let you in."

"No problem." Max opened his wallet to display his FBI badge, and David seemed satisfied, so Max was invited into the apartment. He was definitely nervous and visibly agitated, and he seemed to have a great deal of difficulty looking at Max directly.

He looked up at Max and blurted out, "What's this all about? I hope you aren't here to bug me about my back taxes. I'm out of work right now, and I can't pay them."

Max found himself resisting the urge to assume that David was guilty based on his nervousness, but he flashed a friendly smile. "No, Mr. Johnson, that would be the Internal Revenue Service, and they usually just communicate through the mail. I'm here to ask you a few questions about your former employer, Alligator Enterprises."

David smirked and responded sarcastically. "Former is right. After giving them ten good years, those pricks cut me loose. I was laid off several months ago, and I've been unemployed ever since. The severance package was only a week for each year of service. Cheap bastards!"

Max could see the anger rising up in David, so he tried to defuse it by addressing him calmly and sympathetically. "It must suck to get laid off."

Driven by his anger and frustration, David was finally able to stare directly at Max. "What would you know? Government types like you live off my taxes. You don't have to worry about losing your job. All you have to worry about is when you can sit on your fat ass and start collecting your pension."

Max was becoming annoyed with David's attitude. *I do actually have other worries,* Max thought. *For example, I'd probably lose my job if I beat the crap out of an asshole like you.* But of course, he couldn't say that. Instead, he tried to redirect the conversation. "David, are you aware of the incident that happened this week at Alligator Enterprises?" He watched David carefully as he explained the attacks on the equipment.

David must have realized the seriousness of Max's visit, so he made an effort to calm himself down. "No, I'm not aware of anything like that. Why are you asking me about it? Am I a suspect?"

Max fixed David with his best official stare and pressed further. "Well, you didn't exactly leave on the best terms. And obviously, you're still angry."

David rolled his eyes. "That's for sure. But I'll tell you right now that I didn't have anything to do with damaging their data center. I don't have access to the building any more. I turned in my badge before they escorted me out. Besides, that would be an idiotic thing to do. I admit that I have a short temper, but I'm not stupid enough to do something that would land me in jail. I have enough problems right now. My severance package will run out soon, so I need to find a job pronto."

"How's that going?" Max asked sympathetically.

"How do you think? I just turned 53, and it will probably be impossible to find another good job at my age. Companies treat you like a dinosaur, especially here."

Max didn't respond. After all he was aware of the age discrimination issue, and he really couldn't add much to this discussion. It did, however, reinforce Dave's comments about government employees; Max was not threatened by age discrimination. He mainly had to worry about being shot on the job. Everyone has some cross to bear.

"At any rate, I need you to provide me with a verifiable alibi for the date the attack happened and I will remove you from the suspect list."

David thought for a few minutes as if he was sorting out the information in his mind. "I'll do that. I'll give you the names of my friends who can vouch for me."

"Thanks for your time."

* * *

MAX MOVED ON TO THE NEXT INTERVIEW, William Kane, who had also worked at Alligator Enterprises. William lived in South San Jose and agreed to meet Max at his apartment. William greeted him at the door dressed in a threadbare green polo shirt sporting an IZOD logo, seemingly part of an old, once-stylish fashion. He also appeared to be in his early fifties. He was tall and thin and probably a dedicated jogger based on his fit appearance. William was showing male pattern baldness which didn't help him when having to deal with the age discrimination issue. Also, in contrast with David, he wasn't particularly discomfited by Max's visit.

Max had the same basic conversation with William about identification, layoffs, and Silicon Valley discrimination. He left with William's promise to provide an alibi. So, two down and one to go. His intuition was that in spite of his initial suspicions about David, these two guys were probably innocent, but the alibis were needed to confirm that.

* * *

THE THIRD INTERVIEWEE OF THE DAY was Alfred McCandless. Alfred had moved to Palo Alto after his firing from Gigabit Western Networking Corporation. Max recalled that Alfred had been terminated for striking another employee, so on the off chance that he might get violent, Max requested to meet him at a Starbucks in downtown Palo Alto.

Alfred's first question was to ask for Max to show him identification. *A reasonable request,* Max thought again, *but this guy seems a bit paranoid*. Max showed it to him and suggested they grab some coffee and move outside to the patio.

Max briefly evaluated Alfred based on his appearance. He was a husky guy, probably in his early fifties like the others he'd interviewed. He had cropped, black hair and was clad in a short-sleeved Hawaiian shirt, jeans, and tennis shoes. His face bore an intense expression with angry eyes giving him the appearance of having a major chip on his shoulder, but Max tried not to jump to conclusions until he finished the interview.

The short wait for their coffee passed by in uncomfortable silence. Max still had only told Alfred in general terms why he wanted to talk with him. Once they moved outside, Max got right to the point. "Several nights ago," he started, "there was a criminal assault on the lab equipment in multiple buildings at your former employer. It resulted in a tremendous amount of damage; the overall costs may run into the millions. Were you aware of those attacks?"

"No, I have no idea what you are talking about," Alfred replied calmly.

"So, you haven't heard anything about an incident like that?"

"No, why would I? Has it been on the news?" Alfred responded with an innocent expression.

Max shook his head. "No, it hasn't. The company doesn't want it to be made public, at least not yet."

"All I can say is tough shit for them. They deserve it."

Here we go again. What an asshole. "Why is that?"

Alfred was becoming more agitated. "As you must know, those bastards fired me. Threw me out on my ear one day for no good reason."

Max thought that maybe he was getting a lever to pull. "My understanding is that you struck another worker. Isn't that a violation of job conditions in the company's view?"

Alfred reached over and sipped his coffee. "That's their interpretation. The bastard hit me first, and I was just retaliating in self-defense. The boss didn't see the first blow, only mine.

After that, nobody listened to my story, they just tossed me out like garbage. It was an excuse to get rid of me. They just want to bring in younger and cheaper workers."

"You seem to be holding a grudge." Max asked, "Did you take out that anger on Gigabit a few nights ago night by attacking them?" Once again, he watched for a reaction.

Alfred had already guessed where this was going, and he needed to deflect any appearance of guilt. "No way in hell. I'm not a moron. I couldn't get into their buildings even if I wanted to. Security is too tight. It's not even worth trying. I'm a hot head, but I don't have a criminal record and I'm not about to do anything that would land me in jail."

"I assume you can provide a valid alibi for the night in question?"

"Yes, I can."

Max was eager to wrap up the meeting. "Okay. That's all I need for now. I may be in touch with you again if there are any further developments. Thanks for your time."

* * *

THE LAST PERSON ON THE LIST, Richard Parker, was residing in Kauai, so Max called him. As he figured, Richard had a solid alibi. He hadn't left Kauai since he moved there several months earlier. He laughed out loud when Max told him about the attacks. However, he didn't offer much more in the way of information. He did brag about how happy he was living on Kauai and that he had spent that morning snorkeling in the tropical waters near Poipu and was just finishing up a Longboard beer.

Max was envious. And he was also curious. *Richard is supposedly being prosecuted for felony theft of property. How is it that he is able to live in Hawaii?* That wasn't germane to his case so he would just need to let it go. It might be prudent to check with the airlines to make sure that Richard hadn't actually made a visit back to the mainland and lied about it.

For the present, all four potential suspects seemed to be dead ends. Back to square one. He was expecting to receive more names from the HR director at Gigabit.

CHAPTER FOURTEEN

Max met with agents Monica and Jason in his Oakland office the day after his four interviews. He gave them a brief summary of his meetings and seeming lack of suspects. "Well, what have you guys uncovered so far?"

"Not much, Max," Monica answered. "I talked to people at six of the companies on my list. They all had basically the same story about the suddenness and severity of the attacks. And, as you can imagine, they're all completely pissed off about what happened. I certainly can't blame them for that."

"Did you uncover any suspects?"

"Well," she continued, "the companies pretty much universally blame disgruntled employees. They're reviewing information and will get back to me ASAP if they determine any likely suspects, but I'm still waiting."

"Did you ask about whether there were any demands like ransom?"

"None," Monica replied quickly.

"Jason, how about you?" Max asked.

Jason perked up in his chair. "I was able to talk to all ten companies on my list. Must have been lucky. I got essentially the same results as Monica. No suspects yet. And their anger is palpable, even on a phone call. These attacks are unprecedented and frightening—so bizarre."

Max considered that for a minute. "Do your companies subscribe to the disgruntled employee motive?"

"Yes," answered Jason, "that seems to be the consensus. They gave me four names. I've already talked to them and pretty much ruled them out."

Max took some time to stare out the window, gradually becoming more frustrated by their lack of progress. "So, what next?"

Jason and Monica glanced at each other, then Monica spoke up. "I guess we don't have much choice except to keep digging. Hopefully, we'll get the names of some really good suspects if we just keep at it."

Max continued to stare out the window. "You're probably right. I still have a few more companies to contact. You do too. Jason seems to be the only one who's managed to cover all ten."

Jason smiled sheepishly. "I just got lucky. Did them all by phone. And I'm still waiting for a couple of them to get back to me."

Max turned back to Monica and Jason with a puzzled look. "Fine. I was thinking that there's something missing in our analysis."

Monica smiled and glanced at Jason. "It scares me when Max says he's thinking."

Max frowned. "Don't be mean. I think when I'm happy, I think when I'm sad, and sometimes I find myself thinking for no reason at all."

"See what I mean?" Monica clearly enjoyed teasing Max.

Max got serious. "Here's what's been bothering me. Are there really *thirty* disgruntled employees from *thirty* companies who all got mad the same week? Is it a gang of angry laid-off vigilantes who pulled this off? Why now? Was there some trigger?"

"That's an interesting point," said Monica. "I don't know what we might be missing. But the disgruntled employee is still probably the best angle. At least until we hear about any ransom demands. That might indicate some kind of criminal gang."

Tom burst into Max's office carrying a stack of file folders. "Max, this is turning into a nightmare. Here are another twenty-five cases that have been opened since yesterday. They all report the same kinds of attacks as the first thirty."

"You have to be kidding."

"I wish I were..."

"I'll need more help."

"Grab a few more agents. This was urgent before, now it's becoming a crisis."

Max resolved to return to his office to read these new reports and to review the previous ones. He felt he must be missing some key clues.

"Also, I don't think there is any connection, but have you guys been following this COVID-19 situation?"

Jason responded first. "Yes—closely. I'm concerned because Santa Clara County has become a hot spot. As you know my parents just relocated into an assisted living facility."

"Yes, I recall. Is there a problem?"

Jason replied with a worried look. "Not yet—that I'm aware of. But they're in the most vulnerable demographic. And up in Seattle, the early cases and deaths occurred in these kinds of elder facilities. So, as you can imagine, I'm worried."

Max nodded sympathetically. "I get it. It's no secret that the virus is becoming more serious by the day. And it seems that the government's response has been slow and inadequate."

Even though politics was supposed to be left out of the office, Jason couldn't resist adding, "Well, not to get too political on you, I think the president's actions have made it worse. He claimed that it was a hoax spread by the Democrats. That it would disappear in a matter of days. And he later made false claims about the availability of a vaccine, and that a cure was just a few months away. As usual with this guy, none of those things were true."

"I know. He's played fast and loose with the truth for his entire term. Apparently, even a health crisis won't make him change."

"Apparently not. But it's especially worrying because of my personal situation."

"Is there anything you need from me?"

"Mainly I'd like you to be open to giving me a few days off so I can check on my folks."

"I'm sure that can be arranged. I assume your investigative activities can be done remotely."

"Yes. I can accomplish a lot on the road. I won't fall behind."

"Great. Monica, you've been quiet. Is there something on your mind?"

Monica was also worried. "Well, yes, now that you asked. I have two kids in grade school, and I keep hearing rumors about plans to close down the schools the way they have in China and Italy. If that happens, I will have a big problem. My kids are too young to stay home alone, and if they close the schools, I'll have to be home to care for them, or at a minimum split the time with my husband. I can also do some of my work from home, but it might impact my efficiency."

Max thought about the comments from Jason and Monica. "I guess we just have to watch the situation and be flexible. It's not like we have a choice. Nobody can predict exactly where the situation is headed."

CHAPTER FIFTEEN

The next morning, Max got a call from Dave Emerson, the security director at Gigabit.

"Good morning, Max. I promised to get back to you with updates."

"Thanks, I appreciate it. What do you have?"

"Well, here at Gigabit we have a sophisticated NOC. It is located in Building Four, but it monitors events all across the campus. "

"Pardon my ignorance," Max interjected somewhat impatiently, "but what exactly is a NOC?"

Dave gave him a basic overview. "The concept is pretty simple, but the actual NOC is complex. Let me explain. NOC stands for Network Operations Center, a centralized facility that monitors the equipment, applications, and networks. The computers track the health of equipment and networks on the campus. For example, if a server, Ethernet switch, or router fails, the NOC computers log that and report the failure, and usually include the diagnostic cause. It might just be that the server overheated because an internal fan failed. Or it might be a more serious failure like a CPU, memory section, or hard disk drive. But whatever the failure, it would be logged."

Max tried to stay with Dave's explanation, but since he was not particularly technical, it was a stretch. "How do you use the information?"

"It depends. The NOC personnel would see the alarms and take steps to fix things. In some cases, the diagnostic software can automatically fix the problem. Regardless, any failures or errors are logged, and the records are saved for later." Dave followed up with an afterthought. "As an aside, my Security Operations Center is housed in the same facility. It compiles information from the video surveillance cameras as well as badge access events, open doors, forced doors or windows, and the like."

Max was doing his best to follow the discussion, but wondering where Dave was going. "Okay, I understand the setup. How does this help my investigation?"

Dave came to the point. "My staff and I reviewed all available event logs, including security videos, equipment error logs, badge use, and so forth. As you can imagine, the amount of information collected is quite overwhelming, so we spent a great deal of time poring over it."

"Did you find anything? Any clues?"

"No, and that alone staggered us."

"Can you elaborate?" Max asked, still not sure where this was going.

Dave was so familiar with the details that he was surprised that Max didn't instantly grasp the problem, but he continued. "After reviewing all the logs, we didn't find any evidence of unauthorized entry into the damaged areas. In fact, in all cases, the equipment began failing in the middle of the night, and no engineers were present at the time. Beginning around 3:00 a.m., equipment started to show errors at an amazing rate. There was no pattern, just widespread destruction. The alarm panels in the NOC lit up like Christmas trees—an awful scenario. The engineers were overwhelmed because the events were flooding in so fast, they had no way to comprehend what was happening, and certainly no way to fix problems at the rate they were occurring. The incident continued for about four hours and ended on its own. As you know, a huge quantity of equipment was disabled before the incident finished."

Max was still puzzled. "It sounds like this couldn't have been the work of a single saboteur. Or even a small team. How could they possibly attack ten buildings all at once?"

"That's why I wanted to share this information with you," Dave intimated. "Personally, I don't think we're dealing with disgruntled employees."

"Then, what do you think happened? Any theories? I'm all ears."

PROJECT SABOTAGE

Dave felt his next comments would be perceived as a bit crazy, and he wasn't totally convinced that there was a real connection. "One thing we talked about earlier was the strange cockroach incidents in each building. I can't for the life of me figure out how they're related, but the cockroach thing happened the day before the attacks. On the other hand, I've never heard of cockroaches that destroy equipment. Certainly not on the scale that happened in our buildings. But still, I can't help but think there's some connection."

Max had already been considering this coincidence. "Believe it or not, I have thought about that too. Several other cases I'm working on had the same weird appearance of cockroaches the day before their equipment was attacked. Something bizarre is going on. The two things must be related, and I need to shift my focus away from disgruntled employees to the cockroaches. What are the latest reports from the exterminators?"

Dave didn't have much helpful information. "Nothing new. The exterminators say they can't find any evidence that the cockroaches were even here. Nowhere to be found. None in traps, no dead bodies, nor any evidence like fecal droppings. They are puzzled. They even asked me if the story was a practical joke. As you can imagine, that pissed me off a bit."

Max chuckled quietly. "I can certainly understand. I haven't followed through with a lot of companies yet, but I got the same feedback from Alligator Enterprises. They told me that it's as if the cockroaches just vanished into thin air. Their exterminator is stumped just like yours. I guess they plan to just keep searching."

CHAPTER SIXTEEN

J ason, Monica, and Max were sitting in Max's office. Jason said that he'd noticed that four of the companies had reported an odd event at about the same time as the attacks. An infestation of cockroaches had broken out in all four cases the day before the attacks. They only mentioned the cockroaches because the timing was so close to the attacks and initially Jason had thought it was irrelevant.

"Jason," said Monica, "that's interesting because I saw the same thing in five of my reports, but I ignored it because it didn't seem important."

Jason looked at her pensively. "I don't know if it's relevant either, but the timing does seem...odd."

"I didn't notice it in the first reports I read, but that did happen at both of the companies I investigated. In fact, at Gigabit, it happened in ten buildings on the same day—the day before the attacks. I just glossed over it—but now I'm sure there might be something to it."

Jason shrugged. "Cockroaches are a real annoyance if they break out into an infestation, but I've never heard of them causing such damage. I thought all they did was multiply, eat scraps of food, and crap all over everything—disgusting, as far as I'm concerned. They're pretty small, and I just can't imagine they'd be responsible for the kind of damage we're seeing."

Max considered this for a minute. "How do you think they might be connected?"

Jason replied, "Beats me. However, the timing must mean something. In each report, the cockroaches showed up the day before the attacks. Seems like a lot more than coincidence."

Monica brightened up a bit. "Perhaps they were placed there by the criminals as some kind of distraction? Part of the MO? Maybe to distract the security folks?"

"What do you mean?" asked Max.

Monica smiled. "I mean—you drop in a bunch of cock-roaches, then when they call an exterminating company, the technician gains entry because security would let them inside to deal with the outbreak. Sort of a Trojan Horse technique."

Max chuckled softly. "That's an interesting theory, but I see two major holes in it. First, you have to assume that the company calls the exterminator immediately because the attacks all happened during the night of the same day the cockroaches appeared. And second, do you really think the exterminators work an overnight shift? I doubt it. Besides the two companies I interviewed brought in the exterminators the day after the attacks."

Monica thought about that. "I believe you're correct. Jason, are you sure that all the attacks occurred immediately after the cockroaches appeared?"

Jason nodded. "Yes, I'm pretty sure, but I can double-check."

Max added, "Well, strange as the coincidence is, there seems to be some connection between the cockroaches and the attacks. We need to dig deeper. Let's call the companies who haven't been interviewed and find out if they also had a cockroach problem."

The next day his team reported back with the results. The information was both enlightening and discouraging—it turned out that at each and every company on the original list of thirty, there had been a cockroach "event." In fact, in every case, the cockroaches showed up the day before the attacks. No exceptions. The correlation was too strong to ignore. The information was discouraging in the sense that it didn't shed any new light on what was actually going on. No one could explain how small cockroaches could have caused such destruction. That was still a total mystery.

When Max followed up with Alligator, he learned that the receptionist had opened a small box in the lobby and the cockroaches had scrambled out. At Gigabit, boxes had been delivered to multiple buildings on their campus and ended up in the computer labs where they were opened. Again, a flood of cockroaches poured out and scattered everywhere. Apparently, that permitted them to enter secure areas.

But, the most curious aspect of the stories concerned the cockroaches' fate. After the exterminators attempted to deal with the infestation, they reported that they couldn't find any evidence of the bugs anywhere. Max decided his next step must be to talk to the pest control companies. This case was becoming stranger by the hour.

CHAPTER SEVENTEEN

Milton phoned Max urgently. "Max, it's Milton from the FBI lab. I've completed the initial analysis, and the findings are disturbing."

"Hold on, Milton, let me get Monica and Jason."

Once Monica and Jason were present, Max put on his speakerphone.

"Okay, here's the highlights," said Milton. "When I examined the damage, I found a powerful super-acid called fluoroantimonic acid. This acid is wicked. It eats through just about everything it touches—plastic, metal, flesh.... It bored holes in the intake screens, and the internal areas were similarly damaged. The effect on the equipment was determined by what it happened to land on inside. The areas were random, and the most sensitive were exposed circuit boards or wiring. The hard drives, which were covered by sheet metal, showed surface corrosion, but no internal damage."

Max couldn't quite grasp what he was hearing. "So, it was a powerful acid? Why did you think it was so important to call us?"

Milton thought the answer was obvious. "Simple. This acid is extremely poisonous. It can eat into your skin. But the real danger is that one of the breakdown vapors it produces is hydrogen fluoride gas, which is unbelievably toxic—even in tiny concentrations in the air it will cause irritation to your eyes and lungs. But at higher levels it can be lethal within minutes."

Max was startled by this new revelation. "But if that's the case, why hasn't anyone died?"

Milton hesitated. "I can't say for sure, but probably because the attacks occurred during the night when no one was present. Also, the amount of acid was small, and the computer centers exhausted the air quickly enough for people to go in without suffering too much. Perhaps we've just been lucky so far."

"Tell me," said Max. "How did the acid get into the equipment?"

"I can't tell you for sure—maybe someone stood in front and used some kind of squirt bottle to inject it."

Max wasn't sure that made sense. "I thought you said the acid eats through just about anything, including plastic?"

"Good point. I need to clarify—it can only be stored in a specific plastic called PTFE, better known as Teflon. You can't even use a glass container; it'll eat through that."

Max was still not convinced. "This doesn't make sense. If you're correct, then some bozo had to move around the crime scene with a Teflon squirt bottle injecting acid into individual pieces of equipment? That might be possible at a small computer center, but how could it be done over the span of ten sites, like at Gigabit?"

Milton didn't have a good answer. "I guess they'd have to be fast on their feet."

Max was not amused. "Very funny. They'd also need access to all ten sites that same night."

At this point, Monica spoke up. "You told us the acid generates a highly toxic gas. If the attacker was standing right there, wouldn't they run the risk of killing themselves? Seems pretty risky to me."

"Another good point. Perhaps they wore a gas mask?"

Jason couldn't hold back any longer. "None of what you're say makes sense. If this criminal, or a team of criminals, has access to the equipment, why wouldn't they just a bring a big sledgehammer and smash the servers? A low-tech solution like that wouldn't force you to risk dissolving your skin or killing yourself with poisonous gas. Besides, the gas mask wouldn't be adequate, it seems to me you'd need full protective gear. That would be hard to conceal."

Milton could tell that he'd stirred up a lot of confusion and doubt. "All good points. Like I said, I really don't know how these attacks were actually done. I just know that they used fluoroantimonic acid, and I really needed to warn you. By the way, I should add that I also analyzed the brown blobs the forensic team sent. Really interesting, though I can't figure out how they fit into the overall picture."

"What do you mean when you say they were... interesting?"

Milton gave them a relatively detailed explanation, which he hoped would be clear and not add to the overall confusion. "Well, they turned out to have been dissolved by the fluoroantimonic acid, hence the deformed globs of debris. But, chemically, they contained a lot of different compounds and elements. I discovered several types of plastic and ceramic material, and traces of lithium, copper, silicon, boron, graphite, and gold. Plus, when I analyzed the small white pellets in some of them, it turned out that they were Teflon."

Max was impressed by the details, but he wasn't sure what Milton was driving at. "Thanks for the chemistry lesson, but what do you think it means?"

Milton ventured a theory. "I think the small white pellets are some type of storage container for the acid. Don't know for sure."

"What about the other materials?"

"I don't know."

Max was mulling this information. "Refresh my memory. Where were the blobs?"

"Mainly on the floor." The team heard him rustling his papers and typing something. "Typically, in front of equipment that had been damaged."

Max wasn't sure why he asked this next question but somewhere in his mind he had a vague theory of his own. "When you opened up the equipment in your lab, did you find any globs inside?"

"None."

"The mystery keeps growing. Is there anything else we should know?"

Milton could only add, "No, I think I covered everything."

After they hung up, Max turned to his team and asked the obvious question. "What do we need to do about these potentially lethal attacks?"

Monica spoke up. "I think it's obvious. We have no choice but to issue a press release warning people of the threat of these attacks, what to be aware of, and how to stay protected. We have no idea where the next attacks will occur, so we'll need to put out warning information as widely as possible."

"*We* don't really know what's happening. What do we say?"

"It seems pretty straightforward to me," she said. "I'll get on it right now. When I have a draft, do you want to review it?"

"Sure, but if I'm unavailable for any reason, just go ahead with it. I trust your judgement."

Monica smiled at the compliment as she left the room to get started.

CHAPTER EIGHTEEN

FBI Press Release, San Francisco Media Office March 20, 2020

FBI San Francisco Warns Companies of Data Center Sabotage

Criminals are targeting data centers at companies in the Bay Area causing destruction to computer equipment.

THE SAN FRANCISCO DIVISION of the Federal Bureau of Investigation is seeking to warn companies that criminal actors have managed to infiltrate many companies in this area and cause significant disruptions.

"The FBI has seen an increase of these attacks in recent weeks. The Bureau wants to help companies protect themselves," said Special Agent Maxwell Smart. "In partnership with our local law enforcement, we will investigate any suspected incidents and bring the culprits to justice."

Generally, the attacks follow this pattern:

Attackers gain access to the data center through forged credentials or accomplices.

They spray a strong acid into the equipment which disables it and takes it out of operation.

These attacks occur in the middle of the night.

The destruction we have observed has been extensive. At the moment, we do not think these are acts of terrorism but we are investigating all angles. So far, no persons have been harmed, but heed the warning at the end of the next section about the possible presence of poisonous gas lingering at the crime scene.

The FBI recommends that companies take the following measures:

Review and update all data center security protocols. Be sure to remove or disable any access badges from former employees.

Many attacks have been preceded by unexpected packages. These can be either plain boxes or boxes labeled as computer equipment. Do not open them under any circumstances.

If you are suspicious of a shipment you have received, contact us immediately.

Watch for unusual activity, for example, individuals accessing your data center who have no legitimate reason for being there.

If you have suffered from an attack and you detect any odd odor in the data center, vacate immediately. In some of the attacks, a highly poisonous gas remains for a short time. This warning must be taken absolutely seriously.

Report incidents to the FBI or your local police department.

Report suspicious activity to the FBI local office in Oakland, which is leading the investigation. You can report it to our website or by calling 415-704-TIPS.

PART III

CHAPTER NINETEEN

MID-NOVEMBER 2019

About four months prior to the first data center attacks in the Silicon Valley, the senior agent within the Ministry of State Security (MSS), casually referred to as the General, was standing quietly in his fourth-floor office gazing out the window. His actual name was Liang Xaobai but within the MSS he was called the General out of a perverse acknowledgement of his reputation and authority. He was known to be highly efficient and ruthless in his dealings.

Looking down at the Guangzhou cityscape below, the General was amazed by the magnitude of changes that had occurred in his hometown, where he'd lived for over 60 years. New buildings were interwoven with traditional small businesses, including shops and restaurants as well as pharmacies and medical offices. Guangzhou was now a hub for Chinese culture and education, as well as a manufacturing center for products shipped throughout the world. It was conveniently located near railway lines, major highways, ports, and airports, and not far from other key cities, such as Hong Kong, Macao, Foshan, Shenzhen, and Dongguan.

He was not a particularly sentimental person, but he had to admit that he was quite proud of how his hometown had evolved. In addition to all the cultural and business features, Guangzhou provided tremendous opportunities and resources for his various projects.

Gazing out at the community park across the street also dredged up memories of the times he had played with his young children and walked there with his wife which only further enflamed his desire for revenge. His family had been killed by the Americans when they shot down a Chinese commercial airliner over the South China Sea. The Americans claimed it was a tragic accident, but the General never believed their story and vowed to seek revenge. Project Inferno had been his first attempt.

Project Inferno was designed to ship modified toy robots into America that would ignite and wreak havoc in the homes of his sworn enemies. It was an unauthorized covert program set up by the General and run by a small team. It had unraveled quickly because his team of MSS agents had become quite sloppy and had been discovered by the American FBI. The project was initially successful but had to be ended abruptly once they were discovered. He had carefully eliminated all evidence, including agents as well as labs and manufacturing facilities, and the executives involved at those companies.

He had avoided blame for Project Inferno because once it was uncovered by the Americans, the Chinese government denied all knowledge of its existence and refused to accept any responsibility. That was still the official stance, and though it initially had caused a diplomatic uproar, the Chinese government still denied it and gradually the furor had subsided. The cover-up was apparently successful, since the General had not been associated with the scheme, let alone blamed for anything. And nobody in the government was particularly interested in solving the issue. For one, it was an unauthorized project. And secondly, since it had been stopped by the Americans and denied by the Chinese government, nobody wished to dredge up further investigations. Their attitude was to simply let sleeping dogs lie.

Unbeknownst to the General, there was another key development on the horizon that would undoubtedly help him stay hidden from blame: the coronavirus outbreak. That epidemic would originate in Wuhan a mere 400 miles north of Guangzhou. The COVID-19 pandemic that began in December 2019 would infect more than 84,000 Chinese people, cause more than 4,600 deaths, and persist well into March 2020 before it was seemingly brought under control. That medical emergency in China had expanded over a wide area. It was a threatening situation that had demanded the undivided atten-tion of the authorities. It resulted in massive lockdowns and disruptions that affected tens of millions of Chinese citizens. It provided a good deal of distraction. Of course, nobody knew these events were on the horizon in November 2019.

So the General had managed to launch his secret Project Inferno and not get caught. However, because the project had been terminated prematurely in his mind, he wasn't finished. Even though the project had successfully inflicted consider-able physical and economic damage and killed a number of American citizens, he considered it just a start. He continued to hold the Americans responsible for the death of his family.

He wasn't sure what form a new attack would take. He was clever but short on new ideas. He knew that the attacks must not be obvious. In other words, he couldn't just use the mili-tary to directly attack America. That would be too blatant and in the long run, if a conflict escalated, the Americans would emerge victorious. Overall, the Chinese military was greatly outclassed by the Americans. Also, a real military move would be hard to contain and truthfully, he didn't have sufficient sup-port or allies within the military to make such a move.

Biological weapons were a possibility. He could find a way to introduce pathogens into America that could be extreme-ly effective—witness the latest outbreaks of Ebola or AIDS. COVID-19 had spread quickly even though it was not inten-tionally released by the Chinese. Plenty of conspiracy theories were flying around the world claiming that the coronavirus was actually a Chinese bio-engineered project that had accidentally gotten loose. Even if that were true, and the General had no reason to believe that it was, these viral outbreaks illustrated a key drawback with using biological weapons. They are too difficult to control. Once released, they travel quickly and will ultimately backfire. Some other conspiracy reports out of Russia even claimed that the Americans were responsible for the creation and release of COVID-19. In truth, the novel coronavirus probably jumped from an animal, such as a bat or pangolin, to a human host at one of the live food markets in Guangzhou. It was a case of "spillover" as epidemiologists often feared. The General quickly ruled out biological weapons.

Cyber warfare could be an option. These attacks might be effective, but since they had become so commonplace from independent hackers as well as state actors, most governments and companies were devoting enormous resources to blocking them. It had become a new "cold war" with attacks and responses from both sides. Also, the Chinese military already had set up an organization of thousands of computer hackers to work on their behalf in numerous internal groups. So the General would only be duplicating their efforts which might be useful but not particularly creative.

He did make a mental note of the news concerning the Equifax hack that the Chinese military had pulled off a few years prior. The information that was stolen included personal and financial data for over half of the American population. He reasoned that that information could be useful for identifying Americans who might be susceptible to coercion, to be re-cruited to surreptitiously support his new project. That notion could be explored later.

His first requirement was to find an agent to lead his new project. During Project Inferno, he had used an experienced MSS agent named Zhang Wei, usually referred to by his nick-name, Colonel X., an aggressive and efficient agent. He was a trained engineer, whose experience had been a tremendous asset for managing the technical aspects of Project Inferno. The project had gotten off to a good start but unraveled after about six months.. Sadly, after Colonel X died one sunny day in an apparent robbery, nobody within MSS seemed to ques-tion his fate. Apparently, he didn't have many friends or rela-tives, or else people just instinctively knew to look the other way. At any rate, he was a non-factor now.

For this new project, the General also decided he would seek approval from the higher-ups. He wasn't sure how to ap-proach that, but it might be worth the effort to try to achieve some form of legitimacy. He would need to handle it delicately, as there were only a few government leaders he could trust.

He began reviewing resumes of MSS agents who might be good candidates. A few of them jumped out, in particular the resume of Mai Lin Chang. She was an agent in the Information Management department. She had been employed by MSS since she had graduated from Guangzhou University about twelve years earlier. She had scored extremely high evaluation marks for efficiency, loyalty, patriotism, organization skills, and ability to work closely with other agents and had been involved in some secret operations, one of which was actually in the U.S. That experience might be helpful, though he visualized that her possible role as a team leader would keep her here in Guangzhou. Her team at large might travel to America, but it didn't seem necessary to the General that she travel. In fact, it would probably be too risky.

Mai had several other characteristics that also appealed to him. She was young and energetic. She was ambitious and eager to get ahead in her career with MSS. And she was single with no family to distract her, so she would undoubtedly work long hours. The General had his secretary set up a meeting with her the next day in his office, so he could evaluate her in person.

CHAPTER TWENTY

INTERLUDE: EPIDEMICS AND PANDEMICS

While the General was pondering his next plot, he had no way of knowing that a pandemic was beginning to develop. Subsequently, this pandemic would affect people around the globe, and it would also interfere with his plans. But he didn't have any knowledge of what was coming.

Some background information may be helpful for putting into context the relationship of the coming pandemic to this story. Humans have periodically suffered from the effects of infectious diseases. Many disease agents could be responsible, including bacteria, viruses, or single-cell parasites. The main difference is that an epidemic is localized to a relatively small geographic area whereas a *pandemic* refers to an outbreak that occurs widely, perhaps encircling the globe.

Sometimes the word "plague" is used as a synonym for "epidemic" or "pandemic." The most infamous plague was caused by the bacteria *Yersinia pestis*. This disease was responsible for several of the worst plagues in human history including the Black Death (1346–53) which is estimated to have killed 75 to 200 million people across three continents, and the Plague of Justinian (541–42) thought to have killed half the population of Europe at that time, about 25 million people. In the ancient city of Constantinople alone, it was killing 5,000 people a day during its peak, and ultimately about 40 percent of the city's population perished.

Bacteria were responsible for two other major plagues: The Third Cholera Pandemic (1852–60) and the Sixth Cholera Pandemic (1910–11). Cholera is caused by the bacteria *Vibrio cholerae* which is ingested through contaminated food or drinking water. Symptoms are severe diarrhea and dehydration. It is often fatal. The Third Cholera Pandemic killed about one million people in Asia, India, Europe, North America, and Africa. The Sixth Cholera Pandemic mainly affected the Middle East, North Africa, Eastern Europe, and Russia ultimately killing over 800,000. By 1923, cholera was brought under control by improved sanitary conditions in major cities, though it is still endemic in India.

While viruses are biologically different from bacteria they have caused many of the worst pandemics in human history. Most of the worst pandemics have been caused by some version of the influenza virus. The worst four flu pandemics on record (described by date) include:

The "Asiatic Flu" or "Russian Flu" (1889–90), which was discovered to be caused by the influenza subtype H3N8. Its exact origin is controversial because it seems to have originated in three separate locations simultaneously. Regardless, it spread rapidly, and in the end claimed the lives of over a million people.

The so-called "Spanish Flu" of 1918–20, which is a misnomer. This flu strain actually originated on a U.S. Army base in Kansas, but when a huge number of people in Spain contracted it and the Spanish press wrote about it, the public incorrectly assigned it the name "Spanish Flu." This pandemic infected about 500 million people worldwide and killed about 20 to 50 million individuals. The mortality rate was estimated to be 10 to-20 percent, which is quite high for the flu. It was also unusual in the sense that it struck down hardy and completely healthy adults and often spared children and the elderly. It has been hypothesized that the reason for this is that people with strong immune systems had an overreaction in which their own system attacked and killed them. The term "cytokine storm" is used to describe this immune system reaction.

The "Asian Flu" (1956–58) was a pandemic outbreak of the H2N2 flu subtype that originated in China. During its two-year duration, it traveled to Singapore, Hong Kong, and the United States. The death toll varies, depending on the source cited, but the World Health Organization (WHO) estimates approximately 2 million deaths worldwide, and 69,800 in the U.S. alone.

The "Hong Kong Flu" (1968) was caused by the H3N2 strain of the Influenza A virus, a genetic offshoot of the H2N2 subtype. The first reported case was in Hong Kong and within three months it had spread to the Philippines, India, Australia, Europe and the United States. While it had a comparatively low mortality rate (0.5 percent), it still managed to kill over a million people, including 500,000 in Hong Kong alone, representing about 15 percent of its population at the time.

One of the most insidious diseases of recent history is the HIV/AIDS pandemic with a cumulative death toll of over 36 million people since 1981. HIV/AIDS originated in the Congo in 1976, and currently there are between 31 and 35 million people living with HIV, the vast majority in sub-Saharan Africa where the infection rate is about 5 percent. As public awareness and understanding has evolved and new treatments have become available, many of these people are able to lead productive lives. There has been some lessening of the impact of HIV/AIDS in that the global annual death toll between 2005 and 2012 dropped from 2.2 million to 1.6 million. HIV/AIDS is also somewhat different from other pandemics in that it is a slow-developing disease that can take decades to cause disability and death. And early on, it was associated with the homosexual and injecting drug user communities, and thus was largely ignored by medical communities around the world.

Which brings us to the latest pandemic, the "novel coronavirus" that began in late 2019 and was rapidly spreading worldwide in 2020. This virus is related to SARS (Severe Respiratory Syndrome) caused by the SARS-COV-1 virus. The terminology can be confusing, but the new virus is called SARS-COV-2, while the disease it causes is referred to as COVID-19. SARS-COV-2 is one variant of the hundreds of coronaviruses, some of which cause the common cold. COVID-19 has been described by some people as being totally unprecedented, which is ignorant. Just look at the pandemics described above. The only thing that makes it unprecedented is that it is a new virus of the coronavirus family. Its ability to spread widely, infect large numbers of people, cause a widespread death toll, and totally disrupt our lives are not new issues.

Some of the initial unknowns about COVID-19 have gradually been answered by the medical community. A new disease like COVID-19 is disturbing because, like all other pandemics, it arose unexpectedly, spreads indiscriminately, and kills. But, it is not unprecedented. Unfortunately, it is just the latest pandemic in a long list that have periodically devastated the world population. It's not the first, and it certainly will not be the last.

It should be noted that the true pandemics listed above are only some of the worst that have occurred. Over human history there have been many other epidemics that have caused serious death and misery. Recall that the difference is mainly a matter of geographic spread. Devastating epidemics have been caused by diseases like smallpox, yellow fever, measles, typhus, cholera, plague, poliomyelitis, malaria, dengue fever, hepatitis, meningitis, MERS, SARS, Zika, Chikungunya, and Ebola, to name a few. Many of humanity's historical epidemics killed thousands or millions of people, but by definition were localized.

There are numerous other examples, but the point is that infectious diseases have been with us for our entire human history. One thing that seems new is that many of the latest diseases are "zoonotic," which means that they are diseases that normally live harmlessly inside some wild animal host but jump to humans at some point. Once in humans, if that disease can then move from human to human, it can be devastating. Diseases like HIV/AIDS, MERS, SARS, Ebola and COVID-19 have made this jump. Some epidemiologists think that these events are becoming more and more common as human populations steadily expand and intrude into native habitats. There's growing evidence that as native habitats are gradually destroyed and humans come into closer contact with animals like bats and rats, these host animals are the vectors that pass the disease to humans. The process even has a name: spill-over. And these experts predict that these events will occur more frequently in the future.

Why bring up this discussion of pandemics? Simply, the COVID-19 pandemic will have significant implications for the new revenge plot that the General planned to roll out. The impending lockdowns and factory closures in China will greatly impact his ability to execute his plans.

And the COVID-19 pandemic will also have far-reaching social and economic impacts on the FBI and other participants as they try to investigate the General's unfolding plot to determine its effects and origins.

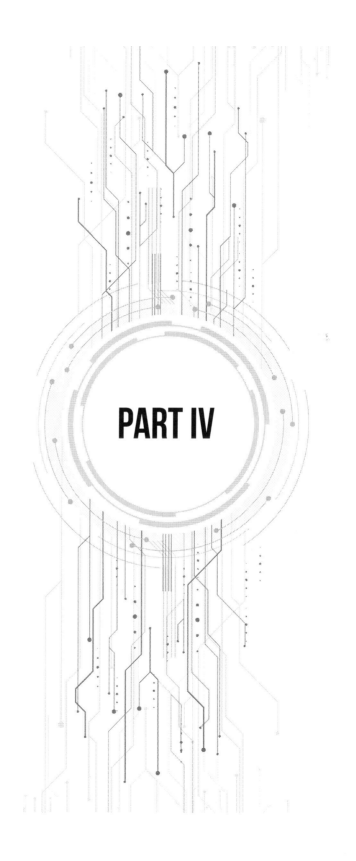

PART IV

CHAPTER TWENTY-ONE

NOVEMBER 15, 2019

Headquartered in Beijing, the Ministry of State Security (MSS) is responsible for counterintelligence, foreign intelligence, and internal political security. The U.S. Department of Justice has likened the MSS to a combination of the CIA, NSA, and FBI. MSS's mission is to ensure the security of the country against enemy agents, spies, and counter-revolutionary activities designed to sabotage, destabilize, or overthrow China's Socialist system. Its logo displays the Communist party emblem instead of the state emblem that most other Chinese government agencies use.

MSS has a sub-headquarters downtown in the government district of Guangzhou. It's an imposing building with surprisingly little to indicate its affiliation other than a small MSS logo on the front facade. While the MSS is not exactly trying to hide, they don't seem to feel that their reputation requires showiness. Everyone knows exactly who's inside the building. However, if there is any doubt about the seriousness of the activities of the MSS, all you need do is look up at the vast array of antennae on the roof that bristle all across the roof pointing in various directions.

Mai Lin Chang entered the General's office somewhat tentatively; she was a bit overwhelmed by the meeting invitation since she had never interacted with the General. The General looked up to see an attractive young woman, about 35 years old, wearing a tailored business suit. She had short clipped black hair, modest makeup, and a gold necklace. The General could sense her unease as she fidgeted in front of his massive wooden desk. Prior to the meeting, he had reviewed her resume and had already decided that she was the candidate he would select. Of course, he wouldn't let her know that at the outset.

He greeted her with a friendly smile. "Hello, Mai. Thank you for agreeing to meet with me. Please have a seat."

Without being too obvious, she scanned the room for clues to evaluate the General. The room was sparsely appointed; apparently the General liked to keep things simple since in addition to the expensive desk there was simply a telephone, some bookcases, a few extra chairs, and a laptop open in front of him. Even the walls were minimally decorated with just a few pictures of the General posing with key government officials, including the Party Chairman, Xi Jinping. To one side of the office there was a portrait of Chairman Mao on a red painted wall, which brought out the red stars on his uniform. On the right side of his desk, there was a framed picture of a middle-aged woman and two children. Mai was not aware that the General was a family man, but she considered it impolite to ask about the picture.

The General himself was a small, elegant-looking man, dressed formally in a wool business suit, silk tie, and cotton shirt. He looked like a typical businessman—a banker, if you had to make a guess. However, his affiliation with MSS could be seen in his red-and-gold lapel pin. Mai guessed him to be about sixty years old, but it was hard to tell because he had a round youthful face with no wrinkles.

The General noticed her looking around the room and nodded at her inquisitiveness. "I assume you are curious about why I wished to meet with you."

Mai was eager to get to the point, so she shifted in her seat and replied, "Yes, General. It's not often that I have the opportunity to meet with someone as important as yourself."

"You flatter me too much. Let me get right to the point. I've been reviewing your career here with MSS, and I'm impressed with your qualifications. I think you would be the perfect candidate to run a project that I'm setting up."

Mai looked directly at him. "Thank you for the kind words. Please tell me what project you are talking about."

The General changed to a more serious tone and locked Mai with a steady stare. "First, I want to emphasize that whether or not you decide to work with me, what we confer about here is not to leave this room. You cannot discuss it with anyone inside or outside MSS. As a trained MSS agent, I assume you understand the reasons for my secrecy, and I appreciate your commitment. Is that clear?"

Mai was surprised to hear this sudden change in the direction of the discussion but did her best to hide her reaction. "Absolutely, General. You can count on me to be silent, discrete, and loyal."

Satisfied with her response, after a short pause the General continued. "Here's a brief overview of the project. We will be attacking the United States to exact revenge for their many past crimes. I need someone to lead a team that will design and carry them out. You would be responsible and would manage them from Guangzhou. If necessary, we will provide you with appropriate outside facilities to run the project."

The General paused to let his comments sink in, but when Mai didn't betray any reaction he continued, "I expect this project to be secret and clever, but devastating in terms of damage to the U.S. economy. I'm not really looking for a project that will cause extensive physical damage, although that is certainly alright, but something that will exact a costly toll on their productivity and economic strength. For fairly obvious reasons, you should understand that these attacks cannot come from the military. Nor can they simply be cyberattacks because there's already a team of hackers in our military to perform cyberwar on the Americans. I don't want to duplicate their work." The General briefly stared out the window at the cityscape beyond. "If you accept this assignment, I will expect you to design and develop the exact type of attack that we will be used. Of course, I will offer you some guidance. However, it's ultimately up to you to be creative and perhaps devious and design an attack that is subtle, hard to predict, but effective. It must be designed to fly under the radar of the Americans as long as possible and be difficult for them to figure out and stop." The General paused at this point to let his words completely sink in.

After a few minutes of contemplation, Mai responded with a slight frown. "So you wish to initiate some kind of attack, but you can't even tell me what?"

The General chuckled quietly and had to stifle a smirk at the obviousness of her question. "That's correct. I want you and whatever team you select to come up with proposals."

Mai took a short time to look out the window before responding a bit more assertively than she should have. "So, in essence, I would be accepting this job with blinders on. How can you expect me to be successful?"

The General was not prepared for such a direct and insubordinate response, so he had to work hard to suppress an angry flareup. After taking a short period to calm down and gather his thoughts, he replied, "I've provided you with the project objective—which is quite ambitious. How you implement it would be under your control and would give you a tremendous opportunity to shine within MSS."

Mai reminded herself that she was talking to the lead agent within MSS, and that it would be prudent for her to be careful. "Thank you for the clarification. I meant no disrespect. As you may have read in my personnel file, I have a tendency to speak my mind. In the past, that's gotten me into trouble with superiors. I certainly wasn't intending to be insubordinate, nor to question your plans or motivations."

The General simply acknowledged her comments with a quick nod and then moved on. "Can I count on you to join this project as team leader?"

Mai stared at the table in front of her, pondering the General's offer. In her mind, she was evaluating the pros and cons, but she knew she couldn't stall for long. Even though she had minimal information, she knew it would be bad for her career to turn him down. The General was staring at her expectantly, trying against his natural inclinations to stay calm and patient. It was clearly hard for him.

After a few moments which seemed to drag on for an eternity, she responded, "Yes, General. I accept this offer. When do you want me to start?"

The General's mood lightened up almost instantly, "Thank you. I was hoping you would accept because you are the perfect candidate for this job. As far as I'm concerned, start immediately."

At this point, Mai realized there was no turning back. "What do you wish me to do?"

The General had thought this through well in advance. "The first activity you need to do is to recruit a team. I think you will need about three to five people to start. My preference is that you recruit them from within MSS, however you may bring in some outsiders if they happen to better suit your needs. Again, that's up to you. But if you do want to talk to outsiders, you'll need to include me in any interviews. In fact, maybe you should do that for internal candidates as well. Is that clear?"

"Yes, General. I'll keep you in the loop. Once I've recruited my team, what tasks do you want completed at the outset?"

"As a group, you must determine the nature of the attacks—what kind of weapon you will use."

Mai looked at him with a puzzled expression and asked, "What do you mean by *weapon*?"

"Let's not be coy about the terminology," he said as he looked out the window. "Regardless of the specifics, it will truly be a weapon, no matter the form. We will be waging *war* on America. It will be highly unconventional and sneaky. If the project is executed efficiently, the Americans will not really be aware of the nature nor consequences of the attacks. At some point, I have to assume that they will figure it out and rush to stop us. They will certainly become aware of the high costs. However, we'll certainly know what destruction we have caused, and therein lies the satisfaction for our efforts."

Mai felt a bit chastised. "Yes. I understand your logic. Can you help me by providing a list of possible recruits?"

"Of course. If you tell me what type of individual backgrounds and experience you want, I can work with our personnel department to pull a list of candidates."

"Off the top of my head, I'd say that I prefer agents with at least five years of experience within MSS so I don't have to babysit them. A team with enough knowledge to navigate the MSS bureaucracy. In addition, they need to be well-versed in technology, particularly in the areas of Internet functionality and computer and software design."

"Fine. I'll have personnel sort through their files and provide you with a list of candidates by tomorrow. Do you have any questions for me at this time?"

Mai could tell from his shifting mood that the General was eager to wrap up the meeting. "Not really, but if I do think of any questions later, how should I contact you?"

The General looked directly at her as if to emphasize his points. "Considering the security requirements of this project, you should not email or text me, nor leave any voice messages. The best bet is for you to contact my secretary and set up a brief one-on-one. We could set up a schedule of recurring meetings to periodically review our progress and deal with questions."

Mai simply nodded at his reply. "I understand. Periodic meetings would certainly be useful."

Since she had already accepted the job, it was too late to ask the one question that was beginning to nag at her. She wanted to ask if this project was officially sanctioned and approved. It bothered her that he wanted to use only untraceable forms of communication. On the other hand, the General would undoubtedly just say that it was official, and she would just have to accept his answer. So, she kept any doubts to herself.

CHAPTER TWENTY-TWO

LATE NOVEMBER 2019

One day after her initial meeting with the General, Mai received a large stack of file folders containing the personnel records of twenty MSS agents. She took several hours to peruse the files and chose ten candidates who showed the most promise. The next step was to interview each of them in person to cut the selection down to three, the appropriate number to start the project. A small team would be more efficient, and she could always add more people later.

Remembering the General's request to be included in the interviews, she contacted his secretary to ask for his attendance.

When the secretary called her back later that day, Mai was a bit shocked by the abrupt response. "The General says that he's too busy to be involved in the interviews. He says that he's confident in your abilities, and he trusts your judgement. You should proceed without him."

So much for keeping the General in the loop. Either this project was not as important to him as he had indicated, or he truly was too busy. She tried not to overthink it. It was actually a compliment to hear that he had such confidence in her.

Mai brought in the first candidate. She needed to provide enough detail to explain what she wanted and determine from his responses whether he would fit her needs. But she also needed to be vague. Considering the secrecy of the project, she could not reveal too much. On second thought, she actually didn't know much herself, so there wasn't a lot of detail to reveal anyway.

"My name is Mai Lin Chang, and I am the team leader for a new, secret project within MSS. I am recruiting a team. You have surfaced as a qualified candidate. I will outline the project, but at this time, I cannot provide you with a lot of detail. Rest assured, this is an important project within MSS and has support from the General and his superiors. Your contribution would be valuable, and it would pay off in terms of your personal career aspirations."

At this point in her meeting, most of the candidates sat quietly waiting for her to continue. She used this pause to make a quick reading of their unspoken responses, that is their body language, facial expressions, eye movements, etc., to get an early gauge of their interest and personality. Candidates that showed too much nervousness were quickly eliminated.

"This team will be tasked with implementing a project to perform attacks on the United States. We'll be responsible for designing a 'weapon' that can be delivered to America and cause widespread disruption and costs to their society. One of the main responsibilities of the team will be to determine exactly what this 'weapon' will be and how it will be used. To be clear, the idea is to attack equipment and infrastructure, not people. However, there is always the possibility that American citizens might be harmed. If that's a problem, I need to know right now."

Again, she paused to take another reading of their reactions to her comments. She made a mental note of the candidates who seemed uncomfortable or hesitant. They would be removed from the list. She didn't want anyone on the team that was unnecessarily squeamish.

After each candidate had time to consider her comments she added, "Since this project is secret, you must understand that you can't discuss it with anyone, even other agents inside MSS. That is an absolute requirement with no wiggle room. If you accept this job you will need to swear an oath to uphold the secrecy of the project. If you break that oath in the future, the consequences will be quite severe. Is this understood?"

Mai asked each candidate to commit by stating, "Yes, I understand." If anyone hesitated, she viewed that as a negative response.

At the conclusion of each interview, she simply asked if they wanted to join the team. She gathered the results and returned to her office to decide on her three team members.

Mai requested another meeting with the General to tell him who she'd chosen, but once again, the secretary informed her that he declined her request. She was told to go ahead with her selections. However, he did want to attend her first team meeting. Mai had the secretary add that meeting to the General's calendar.

CHAPTER TWENTY-THREE

LATE NOVEMBER 2019

Mai was joined in an MSS conference room by the three agents she'd chosen: Jiankang Woo, Wie Yong, and Zhang Li. The conference room was unremarkable with an oblong table in the center with a speakerphone on it, a dozen chairs, and a set of cabinets on one wall that seemed to be empty. The windowless walls were painted off-white, and on two walls there were colorful pictures depicting traditional Chinese landscapes. In the awkward silence, Mai could hear a slight whirring from the overhead ventilation system, but it wasn't loud enough to be a distraction. The General was also there off to the side; his body language and position in the room indicated to the team that they were there to hear from Mai and that he would just be an interested observer.

"Now that you've met each other, let's get started," she said. "I'm quite confident that I have chosen an outstanding team, and I'm eager to begin. I know that each of you is curious about this secret project. General, please feel free to interject at any point if you wish."

The General looked up abruptly as if being startled awake. And after staring at each of the agents, he said, "I will if I feel the need, but for now, this meeting is all yours. Please proceed, Mai."

Mai had hoped that the General would take more of a leadership role. "Thank you." She looked at her new team. "You're part of a secret project that will design and implement attacks on our enemy, the United States of America. These attacks need to be subtle and secretive so we don't get caught, but effective enough to cause significant damage, particularly to equipment or infrastructure. Humans might be collateral damage, but they aren't the primary target. We wish to damage computers, networking equipment, and the like, so that the Americans will have to spend resources diagnosing, fixing, and replacing these items. Any particular attack may not seem that significant, but the overall cost will mount to significant levels."

Jiankang sat upright and posed the first question to Mai. She made a mental note of the fact that he was eager to participate, which she viewed as a positive sign. "You've used the word *attack* several times, but I haven't heard you describe what type of attack you have in mind. What exactly will we be using for these attacks?"

Jiankang Woo was selected for his overall experience within MSS. Of the three, he'd been there longest—fifteen years. He joined right after graduation from Guangzhou

University, and MSS was the only place he had worked. Jiankang was in his late thirties, tall and thin with jet-black hair. He was nervous, high-strung, and tended to shift around in his seat. He also seemed to think he was a Steve Jobs acolyte, since he showed up at the meeting in designer blue jeans, a long-sleeved black turtleneck, and leather sandals. Mai wasn't sure she appreciated his casual appearance, but she wouldn't say anything. One of the reasons Mai had selected him was because he had actually spent some time in America. While attending graduate school at the University of California, Berkeley, he had worked for MSS trying to recruit industrial spies in the Silicon Valley. These efforts were largely unsuccessful because the FBI was carefully monitoring Chinese nationals and had become suspicious. He was eventually quietly asked to leave America—the Chinese Embassy contacted him and sent him home. Mai thought his experience would be useful for helping her establish a shell company and recruiting some local agents or conspirators.

Mai turned to Jiankang. "Yes, you're absolutely correct. I haven't told you what the attacks will entail, and that's on purpose. The General has tasked us with designing it ourselves. Let's drop the pretense. What we are talking about is as an act of war against America. So, let's just call it 'the weapon' until we've narrowed down the parameters. The General wants us to be as creative as possible. Let me read you a list of his requirements:

It needs to be subtle and unexpected. Ideally it might be some-thing that appears to be a normal thing in that environment.

It must be easy to smuggle into the country. That will take some careful thought, since if it is discovered in transit, all bets are off.

It must be more or less undetectable as a weapon. Once used, it would be useful if it could self-destruct to hide evidence.

It must be self-directed and capable of attacking a variety of targets.

It must be something we can produce in large quantities."

After outlining these general requirements, she looked up at the three agents. "So, we have our work cut out for us. I want you to go off and start trying to figure out solutions."

Jiankang spoke up again. "Are there any types of weap-ons or attacks we should rule out?"

Mai was pleased at that insightful question and concluded that Jiankang might emerge as a team leader. "Yes, there are some restrictions. The attacks cannot involve military weap-ons, biological weapons, or cyberwarfare. You need to come up with a weapon that is new, unique, secretive, and effective."

Jiankang looked a bit disappointed. He was thinking *what's left?* but he kept that to himself.

Mai decided to wrap things up. "At our next meeting, we'll have a full-blown think tank to review your proposals, so be prepared. This may sound like you are in school again, but please bring any supporting evidence. We will reconvene in two days."

Wei Yong was staring down at the table, clearly lost in some personal musing, but in keeping with his natural shyness, he didn't speak up. He was an enigma. He was clearly brilliant, but he was the quietest team member. He was a graduate of the South China University of Technology in Guangzhou, where he majored in computer science. Prior to joining MSS about eight years earlier, he had worked as a design engineer for two local technology companies. He was well-versed in both computer hardware and software design. Mai thought he'd be instrumental in figuring out the technical details of their weapon. He had shown up in casual attire—khaki slacks and a polo shirt sporting the logo of Luckin Coffee, a green stag deer on the white background of his shirt. Wei was about 35, prematurely bald, and wore thick, black-framed glasses; he looked like a stereotypical computer nerd. Wei was the only married member of her team and had two young children.

Zhang Li was watching Wie Yong thoughtfully, wondering at his reluctance to speak. However, there was a question she wanted answered. She turned to look directly at Mai. "My expertise is in database design and management. I've never worked on any type of weapon. How to I fit in to the project?"

Zhang Li had been with MSS about eleven years, the majority spent in various information technology departments. Zhang had graduated from Guangzhou University with a major in economics and a minor in computer science. Over the past few years, she had been involved in solving database design issues with the massive video surveillance system used by the Chinese government. This video surveillance system gathered a huge amount of data, and the design issues were difficult to resolve. Zhang had gained the reputation of not only being highly competent, but also creative and innovative. Mai thought Zhang's skills would be particularly useful for managing logistics and developing target lists. She was petite with a moon face and short cropped black hair. She knew to come to the meeting dressed professionally. She was wearing an elegant black and red silk blouse with a floral design and pressed black silk pants and black designer shoes.

Mai smiled. "None of us have worked on weapons. We need to use databases to develop our target lists. And we may use the data stolen by Chinese hackers to identify Americans who can be compromised to help us, with or without their knowledge. Your database skills will be invaluable for helping us sort through the hacked information to find accomplices."

Zhang grinned.

CHAPTER TWENTY-FIVE

EARLY DECEMBER 2019

Mai reconvened her team two days later in the same bland conference room. Even though technically her title was "Major," she didn't mind that her team addressed her by her first name. She figured that the informality would foster better teamwork.

"Mai, the three of us met yesterday to discuss ideas," said Jiankang. "We covered a pretty wide range of options and narrowed it down already so that this meeting would be a better use of your time."

Interesting. Mai thought again that Jiankang seemed to be a natural leader. He glanced at the other two agents with a serious look on his face, eager to be the center of attention. "The weapon has to be mobile to seek out targets, and it needs to be stealthy. We're not talking about stealth in the sense of a fighter plane trying to hide from radar detection.

Rather, we mean that the weapon should be small and unobtrusive. Basically, largely unnoticed by most people. Or, presumed harmless."

Jiankang paused. "We considered small helicopter-like drones that could be outfitted with tiny bombs, but smuggling them into America might be difficult. They would make people suspicious and would be discovered quickly. Also, tiny bombs would probably not cause enough damage. So, we quickly ruled out small drones." He then turned to look at Wie. "Wie came up with a brilliant suggestion. What if the drone resembled a natural animal, like some type of insect? It could be mobile and small. Also, if they were seen moving around a target site, they'd be assumed to be a normal pest. Of course, these drones would have to be crafted to look as much like real insects as possible."

Mai perked up at this idea. It was far-fetched but definitely held promise. "Are there such devices? Are there real examples of drone insects?"

Jiankang smiled like a proud cat who'd just eaten a bird. "Yes. Many labs around the world are working on artificial drones that resemble insects. Most of these labs are working on behalf of military agencies to design insect-like drones for applications like covert surveillance. There's a lot of focus on drones that can fly like real insects. By the way, I will continue to call them drones, but that should not to be confused with the term *drone* used to describe male insects in a colony."

"Okay. Please continue."

"While there are many efforts to design flying insect drones," he said, "the results have been mixed, so we rejected that idea. Most examples can only haul tiny explosives and fly only for a few minutes before they need to recharge their batteries because flight is very energy-intensive. Some labs have focused on rolling bugs with wheels. It's an easier design and can be enlarged. However, for our purposes, it wouldn't look enough like a real insect. So, we ruled them out. We think the ideal solution is to base the weapon's design on a normal six-legged insect, such as a cockroach. They're the ideal size. Small enough to sneak into things but large enough to carry a useful payload. They're ubiquitous. They often cause infestations, so any casual observer might overlook them. I was thinking of the General's suggestion that the weapon resemble something that belongs in the target environment. Cockroaches certainly fit the bill."

Jiankang sat back and waited for Mai's response. She was smiling, so he assumed she was pleased. He glanced at Wie, who looked pretty self-satisfied, but as usual remained silent. After a short pause, Mai spoke up. "Explain a couple things to me. First, how could an artificial cockroach act as a weapon? And where would we find these artificial cockroaches? Who would make them for us?"

"We did some investigating and determined that several government labs are pursuing research into drone insect designs. In addition, there's a local company called New China AI Creations that has created some robot insects in their labs. It's not clear, but they might be funded by the Chinese military. They're state-owned, which means we can probably count on their discretion. But that probably doesn't matter for our purposes as long as they can make large quantities of cockroaches to support our project. Now, to your question about how to weaponize them. We'll build a small container of highly corrosive acid that could be dripped or sprayed onto the target, causing enough corrosion to key components to disable it. There are powerful super-acids that will eat through just about anything, including metals, rubber compounds, human flesh, and other organic materials.

"The acid could be effective for a wide variety of targets. For example, inside a large business building, or a computer lab, they could be programmed to seek out computers or other equipment. The drone cockroach could attach itself to the outside of a device and spray the acid into the intake vents. It would not have to get inside the chassis. Or, even simpler, the drone cockroach could seek out network cables and power cords attached to the equipment and destroy them. The possibilities for causing mayhem and destruction are virtually endless.

"This solution fits the General's need for a highly disruptive weapon that can cause widespread problems for the Americans. They will be driven crazy trying to diagnose problems and replacing destroyed equipment. And, theoretically at least, they won't understand the cause of their issues, at least not for quite a while."

Mai was intrigued by her team's proposal. While it sounded a bit like science fiction, she was vaguely aware that small robotic drones were rapidly evolving. The next step would be to meet with a local company to determine if they could actually build drone insects that would meet her needs. "Jiankang, please contact the people at New China AI Creations and set up a meeting. Be sure to mention that you are calling on behalf of MSS; that'll get their attention. Also, set up meetings with any other government labs you feel would be helpful."

"I'll do that immediately."

Mai added, "There are other issues we need to resolve quickly, such as how would we get these into the States, deliver them to secure target sites, and make them safe for transport? Also, how many can we make? Obviously, there are still a lot of open questions."

"We'll keep working on solutions for you."

"Thanks. That's all for today."

Mai was feeling more and more confident that she'd selected the right team. For example, the initiative they displayed in brainstorming ahead of this meeting was useful.

Their logical analysis of the problem to reach this preliminary concept was also quite impressive. Hopefully, their well-thought-out ideas would result in a true project concept. She could visualize her successful career path steadily unfolding before her.

CHAPTER TWENTY-SIX

EARLY DECEMBER 2019

New China AI Creations was headquartered in a modern office complex in the Guangzhou Free Trade Zone. The building oozed success. In the past, companies tended toward a low-key image, but in the age of the Internet, it was more or less permissible to be a bit showy.

Mai and Jiankang exited their taxi in front of the building. Looking up, they were impressed by an imposing three-story red brick building with large steel and glass windows and doors. It had a logo on a raised sign above the door which both Mai and Jiankang thought was sort of uninspiring. It was simply the name in both Chinese and English, New China AI Creations, in large dark-blue block letters.

They entered into a beautifully appointed atrium lobby, complete with tropical plants and skylights. The walls were adorned with colorful abstract art featuring circuit board designs, clearly intended to reinforce the high-tech business theme of AI. On the far side of the lobby, an attractive young receptionist greeted them, then escorted them down a long hallway to a small conference room deep in the building.

They were met by Li Jun, the CEO; Zhang Qiang, the IT director; Quong Lei Kwan, the head engineer; and Wang Jing, the logistics manager. All four were dressed in black business suits with white cotton shirts and either red or blue silk ties, and to Mai they looked like clones. That was a strange thought that she filed in the back of her mind because it was irrelevant to today's meeting. But none of them stood out.

Mai kicked off the meeting. "Thank you for agreeing to meet with us. Jiankang tells me that he already outlined our needs to you. Is that correct?"

The CEO, Li Jun, naturally took the lead and responded. "Yes, and what he told me is intriguing. We are more than happy to assist MSS."

Mai smiled and jumped right into the discussion. "Before we go into detail, could you share what capabilities you have developed with your robotic miniature animals, in particular insects?"

Li Jun glanced quickly at Zhang Lei Kwan. He was wondering how much these MSS agents knew about their activities. He had to assume they probably already knew a great deal considering the role of MSS, so it probably wouldn't be prudent to hide anything. However, he still felt an obligation to protect his company's intellectual property. He looked at Mai and responded politely. "Mai, a lot of that information would be considered a trade secret, and I don't think I'm comfortable sharing details with outsiders."

Mai smiled thinly and said, "I understand your hesitation. But this is an official MSS request—not just an informal fishing expedition. If it makes you more comfortable, we can sign an official Non-Disclosure Agreement, but I don't think that's necessary. What we want from you falls under the umbrella of national security. This is not a frivolous request."

Li Jun realized that his first instinct had been correct; it would be better for him to comply. He asked, "What specifically would you like to know?"

Mai was confident that she already knew the answer, but she wanted Li Jun to respond anyway. "Have you developed anything like a robot cockroach?" she asked.

Li Jun became more animated. "Yes, as a matter of fact, we have. We've been developing them for the military, who might want to use them as spying devices. It took quite a while to miniaturize the components and figure out how to make it walk with a natural gait. It also required a lot of effort to duplicate the color and movements. It's a project that we are quite proud of."

Mai gave him her best friendly smile. "I'm sure you are. Is it possible to actually see one?"

Li Jun hesitated as if he hadn't anticipated this request. "Yes, I can arrange a quick demonstration for you." He reached over to the conference phone in the center of the table and dialed an internal extension. "Wo Fat, please bring up one of the latest prototype robot cockroaches and give us a quick demonstration... Yes, right now."

About ten minutes later, an uncomfortable-looking young engineer entered the room holding a small cardboard box. He was dressed in a dark blue jumpsuit with the company logo, and he was wearing a badge around his neck. He appeared to be sweating profusely in spite of the air conditioning. He tilted the box he was holding and out of it spilled two cockroaches. They were life-size—about four centimeters long and real-looking. At least, they looked absolutely real to Mai and Jiankang who were certainly not cockroach experts but could easily identify one when they saw it.

Li Jun had waited patiently for the demonstration to start, "Thank you, Wo Fat. Now, please proceed with the demonstration."

Wo Fat pulled a small remote control from his jumpsuit pocket and pressed a few buttons. Immediately the two cockroaches began to move around on the conference table. Mai watched as the robots walked about and explored the environment. Jiankang was entranced and couldn't stop staring at them. The cockroaches roamed across the table crawling over low objects like notepads and avoiding any substantial objects like laptops. As they crawled around the table, the two long antennas on the front of their heads moved up and down and side to side, obviously testing the environment.

Jiankang commented, "I'm no expert on insect locomotion, but their movements seem lifelike."

Li Jun seemed proud. "Yes, their movements are as close to life as we can make them. Their locomotion is based on endless analysis of video recordings of actual cockroaches and computerized gait algorithms. You probably can't tell, but we simplified things by using only the front four legs, not all six. That allowed for simpler gait algorithms, as well as less internal hardware. Unless you were really watching closely, there's no way to tell the difference between movements of our four-legged robots and the six-legged actual cockroaches. Their walking motion and capabilities are almost identical."

Mai was impressed. But she had many more questions. "Clearly you've solved the walking problem. Now please tell me what other capabilities they have. Do you need the remote control in all cases? How would you direct them autonomously? What kind of sensors do they have? How long can they run on a full charge, and do they recharge?"

Li Jun turned to the head of engineering, Zhang Lei Kwan, and asked him to respond.

"No, the remote control isn't necessary. They can operate autonomously. They can be specifically directed or put into a search mode where they will seek out specific objects. As far as sensors, they have rudimentary light sensors—eyes, if you stretch the definition—tactile sensors in the antennas, programmable odor sensors, heat sensors, and sound sensors. When the battery gets low, they seek out a light source and recharge using the thin solar cells built into the wing coverlets on their backs."

"That's amazing that you can cram all that into such a small package," Mai observed. "Two more questions. First, would it be possible to add a small container or vial inside? And second, could you produce these robots in large quantities?"

Zhang considered her questions, looked up at the ceiling for a moment to gather his thoughts, and replied. "Possibly. How big is the container? What's the container for? And when you say large quantities, what exactly to you mean?"

Mai looked over at Jiankang, then decided to reveal some details. "Well, we might as well be up front right now, since you will eventually figure out what we're up to. We intend to weaponize these artificial cockroaches by putting a small vial of super acid inside them to be delivered to targets such as computers or networking hardware. And by large quantities, I'm thinking of hundreds of thousands, if not millions."

Li Jun couldn't help letting out a short gasp. "You want to turn these into weapons? To what end? What or who is the target? And you are talking about mass production which could be costly to set up. Who will pay for it?"

Mai didn't react overtly except to attempt to reassure Li Jun. "Rest assured these will not be used domestically, they will only be used to attack targets abroad. I don't know anything about how to set up mass production, but I'm sure your people do. As far as payment, MSS will be generous in terms of funding. In the long run, I'm pretty certain that this project will be highly profitable for you."

All around the table, there were several quiet sidebar conversations at such a low volume that Mai couldn't hear them or decipher what they were actually saying. But she could see that she had definitely stimulated their curiosity and had given Li Jun and his team a lot of information to digest. So, she offered to end the meeting and reconvene in a few days after they had time to give her presentation some thought.

"Let's wrap up this meeting and plan to reconvene in a few days. At that meeting we can discuss any further specific requirements and talk about the project in more detail. Is that satisfactory?"

Everyone nodded, so Mai and Jiankang got up quickly and exited.

CHAPTER TWENTY-SEVEN

EARLY DECEMBER 2019

Mai's team was assembled again in the conference room at MSS. "Team, it appears that New China AI Creations has the right product, a lifelike robot cockroach that will meet our needs with some minimum alterations. It was realistic looking. We were both quite impressed."

Jiankang nodded and added, "Yes they were quite impressive, though I have to admit that it was eerie to realize that they were actually robots, not real animals. Their design is quite intricate and functionally complete."

Mai interjected, "We need to start making some decisions about how to proceed. For example, we need to figure out what acid we will use. We need to decide what changes we will make. For example, what types of search behavior do we want? What types of targets should they seek? How and when do we direct them to attack with the acid? How will we smuggle them into America? This is critical to our success. If our shipments are discovered, the project will be thwarted. Zhang Li, you have the experience with logistics, so start thinking about how we can import them without getting caught. Wei Yong, you are the most technical person on the team. I need you to research what type of acid would be best. I assume that the stronger and more corrosive it is, the better. But also research the safest handling methods. In other words, how do we store it, as well as how do we protect workers from harm when they are putting it into the robots? It also must be safely contained during shipping; it can't accidentally release. It can only be released at the final attack event. Jiankang, start devising plans for what targets we should pick. That will lead us to figuring out how to set up the search behavior of the robots. I assume we will need different search patterns for different types of equipment. And perhaps we will need the robots to have the flexibility to change targets on the spur of the moment. In other words, depending on their environment, they might attack computers or servers, or switch to cables instead. Zhang Li, I need you to start analyzing the data that we obtained through the Chinese hackers and organize it. That is, we will look for potential accomplices; people we can compromise with bribes or threats. We have a lot of work to do, so please get started right away."

CHAPTER TWENTY-EIGHT

MID DECEMBER 2019

"Jiankang, please update us on the search patterns and targeting methods you propose."

He was pleased to be asked to lead the discussion. "Certainly. Assuming our targets are computers and other equipment, then I think the best approach is to have the robots seek out electrical activity, noise or air currents . Once they have moved close to or onto a piece of equipment, they can refine their activity further. Let's take a computer or server as an example. As you know they generally have fans that create air flow from front to back for cooling. But we need our drones to attack from the outside. They'll only be able to do that effectively if they inject the acid on the intake side so the acid flows inside. Injecting on the outflow side would just cause the acid to be dispersed into the air outside the chassis. So how do you make sure they are on the correct side? It's actually simple. These robots have tactile sensors that can detect air currents. We simply program them to detect whether the air is blowing on their dorsal or ventral side relative to how they are standing on the chassis. Air flow on their backs, the dorsal side, means they are facing into the intake which is where they need to release the acid.

"We can also program them to attack power cords and network cables. I think in the case of power cords, we could use a sensor inside that would detect the magnetic field around the cord. That won't work on the network cables; I think in that case, the robots would just have to detect the shapes they were walking on and grab the cables based on that characteristic.

"I'm assuming that the acid will be placed inside the robot cockroach and that it will be released from the ventral side. That orientation supports both types of attacks. I assume that Wei will tell us how the acid is to be released."

Always a man of few words, Wei spoke up. "Yes."

Jiangkang waited to see if Wei was going to add anything else, but when he didn't, Jiankang asked, "Any questions?"

"Not right now," said Mai. "Wei, tell us about the acid please."

Wei rarely spoke, but once he did, he proved himself to be articulate. "I did extensive research on what are called 'super-acids.' The best candidate for our purposes is fluoro-antimonic acid which is a mixture of liquid hydrogen fluoride and liquid antimony pentafluoride. It is one of the most powerful acids on the planet, capable of dissolving just about anything. Metals. Organic materials. Rubber. It can only be stored in Teflon. It can't even be stored in glass. It will need to be handled carefully, but I'm convinced it's a perfect weapon. We want to achieve the most destruction with the smallest trace of acid."

Wei paused and looked around. "We will need to have it sealed into small containers shaped like gel caps to fit inside the abdomen area, about one to two milliliters at most. We may need to ask the robot designers at New China AI Creations to enlarge the abdomen a bit to accommodate them."

As an afterthought, Wei added, "We can store the acid in the containers under a small amount of pressure so that if the container is punctured, the acid will flow out. The release mechanism would be a small needle that could be forced to puncture the container on demand. The acid would then immediately flow out through the needle and onto the target. We need to assume that the quantity of acid would be adequate to destroy or at least disable a target. Perhaps we should test this in the lab?

"One last thing. I haven't figured this aspect out yet, but I believe we need a way to divert a small amount of acid into the robot so that it self-destructs. I'll keep working on that."

Mai was pleased with what she'd heard so far. Now she turned to Zhang Li. "Zhang Li please tell us about how we can get these robots into the U.S."

"Yes, Mai. I'll be happy to.

"Thank you. Please proceed."

Zhang was happy for the opportunity to share her knowledge and prove her worth to the team. "Actually, smuggling them on the sly is possible but risky. Getting them past customs agents would probably draw too much attention. And if we're caught, the game's over. I think we need to find a way to move them through normal import channels.

"We'll take advantage of the fact that these robots can be hidden in plain sight. Let me explain. They closely resemble small, artificial insect toys that are already sold online. For example, I was able to purchase rubber and plastic cockroaches directly from Amazon yesterday. Clearly, they aren't robots, but they certainly look like the robots we will be using. I think we can ship large quantities of these toys in advance and have them steadily moving through customs, so they get used to the shipments. After a while, I figure they won't pay close attention to future shipments."

Mai thought about this for a moment. "Another option we need to explore is to ship them in an inactive state so that if customs did open a box, the robots will be inert and look just like plastic toys. That means we need to find a way to activate them after they've arrived in America. Jiankang, please work on that process."

Jiankang just nodded and jotted down a few notes.

Zhang made them aware of another obstacle. "It occurred to me that getting them into more secure areas, such as computer data centers, might require a different approach. I was thinking we could package them into cartons that were labeled as computer devices. For example, in a box that would normally contain a server or a router. IT people are always purchasing new devices as replacements, so the presence of unopened cartons wouldn't draw suspicion. The boxes would have to look authentic for this to work."

Zhang continued, "Physically getting them inside the data center is another challenge because these facilities are highly secure. I was thinking that for the largest and most valuable targets we will need to resort to old fashion techniques such as, bribery or coercion."

Then Zhang offered her proposed solution. "As a result of our government's hacking efforts against America, we have access to a wealth of data to help us. Several groups within China such as Black Panda, Stone Panda, and Black Vine have been quite successful at stealing information from companies like Equifax, Marriott, and Anthem, as well as the U.S. government's Office of Personnel Management. We can use that data to develop target lists and individuals who we can compromise at the target business. The stolen data includes things like social security numbers, birth dates, email addresses, street addresses, employment details, income and debts, and credit scores. So we search for people who are late on payments or owe a lot of money."

"The possibilities are really endless and only limited by our creativity."

"Excellent ideas. I can tell you've put a lot of thought into this."

"Thank you."

Mai redirected the conversation. "I think our next step is to reconvene with New China AI Creations and review our plan, including any changes we'd like them to implement. If I understand these proposals correctly, we need to ask for several modifications." Then Mai quickly outlined the changes they would request, which included tactile sensors to detect air flow, light and heat sensors, odor sensors, acid containers, changes to the AI programming, manufacturing, packaging, and shipping logistics.

Mai concluded the meeting. "There will be a lot to cover with them at the next meeting. I have to say that I am pleased with the efforts that each of you has put into the project so far. Your hard work shows well."

"By the way, I want all of you to be present at the next meeting with New China AI Creations so that you can answer their questions and concerns in real time. Thanks again. That's all for now."

CHAPTER TWENTY-NINE

MID-DECEMBER 2019

Mai brought her whole team back to New China AI Creations. In addition to the CEO, Head of Engineering, Head of IT, and the Logistics Manager, all of whom had been at the first meeting, several lead engineers from development and manufacturing departments were in attendance. Mai was pleased with the turnout.

Mai kicked off the meeting, "We believe that your robot cockroaches are almost a perfect fit for our project. We would like to review our plans with you and discuss some possible modifications we hope you can incorporate."

Li Jun, the CEO, spoke for his team. "Please let us know how we can help."

Mai wanted to explore a separate idea before they dove into the heart of the meeting. "Can you describe the type of cockroach that you used as the model for your robot insect? Also, please let us know why you picked that particular one."

Li Jun smiled and replied, "Yes, I can certainly do that. We decided to model our robot insect on the American Cockroach, scientific name *Periplaneta americana*. It's the largest of the cockroach species, typically reaching about four centimeters as an adult. It is ubiquitous around the world from the Americas to the Middle East, and throughout Africa and Asia. The name is a misnomer because it originally came from Africa in the 1600s as a stowaway on merchant ships. We decided to use them because their larger size makes it easier to build in the robotic components. They are also remarkable for their speed and agility. They are incredibly fast. They have been clocked in laboratories running almost a meter per second, which is the equivalent of a human being running about 300 kilometers per hour. When they're threatened, they can disappear quickly."

After letting that explanation sink in he added, "The robot cockroaches we have made cannot achieve that level of speed, but as far as we can tell they reach about a third of it, or 100 kilometers per hour."

Mai was slightly annoyed because she had not wanted so much detail, but she tried not to show it, and responded with a hint of sarcasm which she immediately regretted. "Thank you for the biology lesson. Seriously, we also think that they are quite remarkable and as I said will fit into our project quite nicely."

Li Jun glanced around the table. "Can you give us more detail on your project?"

Mai was eager. "Yes, I am prepared to do that. And after that I want to discuss some specific additional requirements."

Li Jun sat back in his chair in anticipation, and simply replied, "Please go ahead. My whole team is extremely interested and curious, and they understand the confidentiality requirements."

Mai began her overview after looking at her team as if inviting them to add to her explanation if they felt the need. Mai proceeded to explain in great detail how the robot cockroaches would be used to disable computers and networking equipment in American companies. She added that there would be potentially hundreds of thousands of attacks.

As Mai shared many of the specific details, Li Jun was stunned by her description of the proposed plot and could only think to ask with a shocked look, "How do you plan to weaponize our robot cockroaches?"

Mai explained again the use of a powerful corrosive acid to be stored in the robot cockroaches and released at the appropriate time to destroy the target as well as to self-destruct the robot cockroach to hide evidence. She explained the mechanism for its release and added that it had to be handled carefully during the manufacturing phase of the project. She further explained the need to store the acid in Teflon containers.

Li Jun was stunned by these revelations. "That acid sounds dangerous to work with. How do I protect my people?"

Mai considered his question carefully. "I put a lot of thought into that issue. I believe the best method is to have these sealed containers produced off-site in a separate facility and delivered to you in their finished form. That way, your people would not be exposed to the acid."

Li Jun was pleased to hear that Mai had already worked out a good solution. "That should be workable. What's the end goal of these attacks?"

Mai thought the goal was pretty obvious, but she answered anyway. "The objective is simple. We want to cause as much disruption and damage as possible which will ultimately add up to enormous costs for the Americans. In a way you could think of it as a low-level form of war. It also has the added benefit that there shouldn't be any human casualties. That is an important goal for the General."

"While we are on this topic, we should discuss the first modification that we need. These containers will not be large; they will probably be ovule in shape, like gel caps, perhaps one to two centimeters long. Clearly the bigger the better so they can hold as much acid as feasible. Is it possible to enlarge the abdomen area?"

Quong responded, since as head of engineering, he would be responsible for implementing any changes. "Without knowing the exact dimensions of your containers, I cannot promise how much we could enlarge the abdomens. I'll have you work with one of the engineers to determine how much enlargement we could manage. However, I'm sure it's possible. The cockroaches might end up looking a bit obese, but it's unlikely that a casual observer would notice. Even an expert entomologist might assume that they were well-fed specimens. Perhaps from an unsanitary restaurant." That led to several audible chuckles around the table.

Mai was pleased to get a positive response, "We look forward to your feedback. As I said the more capacity the better."

Mai then changed the gist of the discussion, "Now let's turn to the topic of sensors. These are critical to our success. These robots must be capable of detecting light, sound, touch, specific odors and heat. They do not need to be capable of actual vision but they should be able to see light sources so they can seek out dark hiding places. As far as sound, or maybe vibration that sense is needed so they can detect approaching dangers. They need to detect air currents with their antennae. With regard to odors as you know cockroaches are voracious and use their sense of smell to seek out food sources. In our case we don't need that level of sensory complexity. All we need is for them to detect a few key odors such as, pheromones or other chemicals used to lure them into traps. They just need to be capable of avoiding those traps, and we assume that if they can smell them, they can be programmed to go around them. As an aside, they don't need to be able to detect poison baits or pesticides because those would not harm them. The glue traps are the main thing they need to avoid. Robot cockroaches trapped on glue boards could become evidence of our project because if anyone were to closely examine them, they would soon discover that they are not real insects."

Li Jun responded, "The robot cockroaches have rudimentary 'eyes' that are quite capable of spotting light sources. They can determine light intensity, direction and other key information."

"Their antennae are quite capable of detecting air flow and vibrations. As you observe them you will notice that the antennas can be held up high in which case air currents would move them about. That gives the robot information about the direction of the air current relative to its own body. You will also notice that they constantly point their antennas down and touch the surface in front of them. That way they can sense any vibrations."

"As far as odors, if you can provide us a specific list, I'm sure we can incorporate detection of those as well. Overall, it sounds like the list is limited which really helps. Duplicating all the odors that cockroaches can smell in real life would be a daunting task, if not outright impossible."

"Heat detection should be relatively simple as well. We would just need to incorporate some tiny thermistors, probably on the front of the head. We should place at least two so that they can provide directionality for the robot."

"Thank you. Now let's talk about the AI programming. The robot cockroach must be capable of search behavior and programmed to discharge the acid at a specified time. Inside the target environment, the robot must be able to seek computer equipment, and then perform specific attacks. For example, in the case of attacking any computer, we think it must know that it is on the intake side of the air vents so that the acid is discharged into the equipment, not just blown into thin air on the outflow side. If it is attacking a cable it must know when to wrap itself tightly against the cable to discharge acid right on top of the cable.

"Once these robots are loose in a building, I'm not sure how we direct them to computers or other equipment. Perhaps we have them listen for the sound of fans, or other typical sounds generated by devices. I'm not sure about that. We are exploring ways to get these robots directly into the target sites. For example, have them delivered directly into a data center so that once released they will not have to search far; they will already be in the appropriate room. That is something we are still working on. Obviously, different targets will require different approaches."

Li Jun nodded thoughtfully before interjecting, "I'll provide the names of the key AI programmers and get them started on solutions."

Mai was becoming optimistic about how her project was taking shape. "Wonderful. Now let's talk about manufacturing and logistics. Specifically, shipping. At our first meeting, I asked if you could produce these robots in large quantities and you gave me a tentative yes. I still can't tell you exactly how many we need. Clearly the longer the project lasts the more we will require. And hopefully we won't be discovered in America by law enforcement so this project could be long-lasting. I think we will need to have you manufacture a steady stream of these, perhaps up to 200,000 to 300,000 per month. If things go well, those numbers could ramp up."

Li Jun frowned momentarily. "That could be quite expensive. Is funding available for that large an effort?"

Mai brushed off his concerns with a firm reassurance. "You shouldn't worry about that. The General has assured me that the money will be available. As I mentioned this project could be quite profitable for your company. In appreciation of your patriotic support we will make it well worth your while."

Li Jun didn't know quite how to respond, so he simply said, "That's great news. Thank you."

Mai continued, "The devices will be shipped to America as 'toys' via normal import channels. First, we will drop shipments directly into small business locations. Later we may want to package some of them in fake equipment boxes so they reach large data centers or IT departments. We need to continue to work on the details. Attacking highly secure targets will require local accomplices." Mai decided that they really didn't need to know more about that. "That's my problem to solve, not yours.

"Of course, your company will not be involved directly in these attacks," she said. "However, we do need you to handle the manufacturing, packaging, labeling, and shipping for us. I was thinking that if you wish, we could set up a shadow company for these activities to shelter you from future scrutiny."

Li Jun sat back, trying to absorb all that he'd heard. After a moment, he responded. "It sounds to me like you've thought of everything. I like your idea about setting up a shadow company. Even though this project is officially sanctioned by MSS, it would be good to insulate New China AI Creations from direct involvement. Safer for everyone that way."

"You're undoubtedly right. I will relay that request back to the General when I update him on the project. I'm sure he won't have a problem with the idea of a shadow company."

"So, what is the next set of steps?"

"I will update the General and get his permission to proceed. I will need you to get back to me with answers to the open questions from this meeting. I would like you to please look into how and where to set up the shadow company. You are much more familiar with the business aspects than I am. Then we should reconvene in about a week."

"That works for me and my team."

"Thank you. This has been a productive meeting. I think we are making rapid progress."

CHAPTER THIRTY

MID-DECEMBER 2019

Mai was sitting across from the General in his MSS office, unsure of his feelings or thoughts. His demeanor seemed guarded, not as friendly nor outgoing as he'd been in her first few meetings. Clearly, he was preoccupied with something else and appeared to not be entirely aware of her presence. He looked up at her and his visage showed a gradual awakening.

"Hello, Mai. I'm busy. Can you make this short?" His renewed friendliness comforted her. Apparently, distracted attitude had nothing to do with her personally. That was a good sign, so she laid out the project for him.

"Where will you get these robot cockroaches?" he smiled and asked after she gave a detailed briefing.

"General, a local company has already developed robot cockroaches. With minimal modifications, they can be adapted for our project."

The General pondered this explanation. "That's remarkable and quite timely. Tell me what the target sites will be. How will you select them? How will you ensure that the robots reach the target sites?"

Mai outlined the import process and how targeting would work. Then she outlined the manufacturing, logistics, and shipping strategies. She emphasized that a shell company would distance them from the project by adding a layer of opacity to the overall scheme. "Getting the packages inside the business might be a bit tricky," she acknowledged, "but we have some ideas for that. We plan to take advantage of social engineering principles, like counting on people's curiosity to open packages. Or using tricks to get people with security access to deliver the packages, unknowingly in most cases. Highly secure areas such as large data centers will require accomplices."

The General took the opportunity to stare out the window to gather his thoughts. "It sounds like your team has thought this through. I don't need any more details. What steps are next?"

Mai was relieved since the General seemed ready to move forward. "Yes, General. My team worked hard on this project. I should add that Li Jun and his team at New China AI Creations have also been cooperative."

The General smirked at that last comment and added sarcastically, "They should be. They stand to make a lot of money."

Mai let that comment go by without responding. Then she added, "We plan to test the robots to ensure that they work effectively, and to perhaps identify any last-minute modifications. Assuming the demonstration is successful, can we initiate the attacks?"

"Yes. Just update me after the demonstration to confirm that it was successful. And by the way, we haven't discussed this yet, but I have some requirements for your target site list. As you might know, California's economy is huge, and in fact, if California were a separate country, it would be the fifth largest country in the world, not far behind China. Silicon Valley makes up a large part of that overall economy. I want you to limit your attacks to the Silicon Valley area. You can develop a long list of companies, and I'm sure that many would be juicy targets, loaded with equipment. That area is also the principle competition and threat to China's own high-technology companies. Hurting them would help our economy."

Mai immediately thought, *There's a major flaw in the General's logic. Hurting Silicon Valley could backfire on China because of the interconnectedness of the two high-technology centers.* But she thought it would be prudent to keep these thoughts to herself, so she didn't say anything.

However, she did add, "General, don't you think that limiting our attacks to one area creates too much risk?"

"That's possible, of course. However, a previous project became too diffuse, and that caused problems. Please just do as I say and limit the attacks to that geographical area. In a way, it will reduce your workload so you should welcome the restriction."

Mai knew that it wouldn't be good to push back. In fact, the General was right in a way. It would reduce their workload and make it easier to track results.

"I will do that. Is there anything else?"

"Not right now. I look forward to hearing about the results of your demonstration. Good luck with that."

"Thank you." With that, Mai exited the meeting.

CHAPTER THIRTY-ONE

LATE DECEMBER 2019

New China AI Creations had incorporated all of the requested changes and now it was time for a demonstration. Mai kicked off the meeting. "First of all, our thanks to your team for incorporating the modifications we requested. This will be the first time that most of us have seen these robot cockroaches actually working—live, if you will—and we're curious to see how they perform."

Li Jun responded for his team. "Thank you. Most of the changes were minor, a few were significant, but overall we believe we've hit the mark. The robot cockroaches have been thoroughly tested in stages throughout the development process, but we have set up a demonstration that closely resembles a real environment for the attacks. We are eager for you to see the results." He stood up and spoke to all the participants in the room. "Let's adjourn to the auditorium for the demonstration."

They all got up and walked down the hall to a small auditorium and seated themselves in the tiered seats. Usually, this auditorium was used for internal meetings or training sessions; this was the first demonstration to be held there. In front it had a small raised stage where the demonstration equipment was set up.

An area about thirty feet square, centered on the stage, was formed by vertical panes of glass approximately six feet high. Obviously, the enclosure was designed to prevent the robot cockroaches from escaping while still allowing observers a clear view of the action. There were video cameras set up on tripods to provide close-up views, particularly of areas not readily visible to the audience, like the back sides of the equipment. They had installed small cones on the legs of the tripods to prevent the robot cockroaches from climbing up and attacking the cameras, which were operated with a remote control by a small team in a room to the right of the stage. These operators could pan the cameras as well as zoom in. Ten large monitors mounted on the high wall displayed the footage.

The items to be attacked in the demonstration were staged in the center of the glass enclosure. Prominent in the center were three mounting racks that held twenty servers, eight routers, and eight Ethernet switches bolted in. The equipment was mounted securely in the racks facing toward the audience. On the rear side various networking cables and power cords could be seen, in some cases connecting equipment to each other, and in some cases leading vertically to overhead racks. While it was necessary to power the equipment and several power cables were actually connected to the rack above, the networking cables were just attached as a bundle but did not go beyond the overhead rack. Plastic cones were also installed on the power cords to prevent the robot cockroaches from crawling past that point in the demonstration and getting into the ceiling above.

The enclosure also contained two worktables, on top of which sat some computers, as well as two laser printers, two fax machines, and four IP telephones. So it resembled a small office or data center installation and provided a variety of objects to be attacked, as well as hiding places here and there for the robot cockroaches to seek refuge. To add to the challenge, about six roach motels had been strategically placed in the enclosure behind some of the equipment to determine if the robot cockroaches could successfully avoid being trapped.

Finally, a powerful array of exhaust fans had been installed above the enclosure to expel the acid fumes. The vents from these fans were connected to chemical scrubbers on the roof to neutralize the acid. Even in China, conscientious companies were careful not to create unnecessary pollution for their neighbors. Besides, Li Jun did not want any nosy environmental regulators poking around his business.

The top of the enclosure was in fact sealed, and all the seams in the surrounding glass were sealed as well to prevent the fumes from escaping into the audience. The team had taken the warnings about fluoroantimonic acid seriously and weren't taking chances. Unfortunately, the floor of the stage would undoubtedly be damaged, and perhaps the glass barriers as well. Clean-up after the demonstration would need to be done extremely carefully considering the corrosive capabilities of this acid and knowing that even small residual amounts could be dangerous.

Once everyone was seated, Li Jun kicked off the demonstration. "Let's start. Please release the robots."

The start of the demonstration was a bit melodramatic in that a small utility robot inside the enclosure was directed to a cardboard box on the left side of the demonstration enclosure. When it reached the box, it extended its two arms, grabbed the flaps, and opened the box from the top side. Almost immediately, a whole host of robot cockroaches launched themselves into the enclosure. For the demonstration, the box contained thirty of them, a number that the team thought would prove the effectiveness of the concept. How many robots would be released at an actual target site was still under discussion.

Once out of the box, the robots scurried in all directions. Some ran behind or inside equipment as if seeking shelter. Others climbed quickly up the racks of equipment as if exploring their new environment, which was exactly what they were programmed to do. Others crawled inside equipment that had large enough openings, including the printers and fax machines. The teams had made the decision that once the robots were free in a target environment, they should start attacking targets right away. For one thing, the element of surprise was important. But also, they could only operate for about one or two hours before their batteries were exhausted. At that point they would need to seek a light source to recharge, an activity that could be a problem. They might be discovered unnecessarily. So why not just have them attack targets right away and then destroy themselves?

The team had all agreed that this approach would be better, but later they would realize the flaw in this reasoning: if a box was opened at a target site in the daytime and the robots attacked, their activities could be witnessed in real time. That wouldn't be acceptable. So later they modified the AI programming to initiate attacks in the middle of the night based on an internal clock. If the robot cockroaches were released in the daytime, their AI programming instructed them to find hiding places and initiate attacks later that night.

The teams were highly pleased when they saw the drones closely examine the roach motels using their outstretched antennae, then back up and avoid them entirely. No robots actually entered into a roach motel. That was exactly what the teams desired because any robots trapped in a roach motel could provide evidence.

Within no more than five minutes, the robots could be seen all over the demonstration equipment. The first attacks started. One robot had positioned itself motionlessly on the front of a server in the center rack. There was no obvious event, but a small wisp of vapor arose from the area where it was standing. A small amount of smoke started to blow out of the vents on the rear of the server. Then the robot itself started to vaporize, rapidly turning into a twisted glob of remnants that dropped to the floor. On the intake screen of the server there was a newly created, small corroded hole. After another several minutes, the server started to light up indicating multiple malfunctions. This same sequence played out on eight more servers.

Essentially the identical set of events occurred on four routers and three of the Ethernet switches. One of the printers and one of the fax machines were similarly attacked. On the back of the racks, ten network cables were eaten through, as well as one of the power cords. This power cord supported a power strip, so all eight of the devices connected to it ceased operating.

The attacks were over in about thirty minutes when nine servers, four routers, three Ethernet switches, and one printer and fax machine were disabled or destroyed. Overall, a pretty successful and probably expensive demonstration.

Mai turned to Li Jun. "I'd say that was a pretty convincing demonstration. They clearly function as designed, and I must say I'm satisfied with the results. Sorry though, but this must have cost your company a lot of money."

"Yes, we did dedicate a lot of resources, but I have to admit that the majority of the cost came from setting up the enclosure with glass panels, fans, and acid-scrubbing equipment on the roof. In truth, most of the computer gear that you just saw being destroyed was pulled out of surplus. Most of it was obsolete and had already been written off. We didn't mention that at the outset of the demonstration because it would not have altered the observed results. So, in the long run, it wasn't as expensive as it seemed, and well worth it. I agree with you, Mai. These robots we have jointly designed are quite impressive. Devious. Clever. Nefarious. Absolutely effective."

Mai looked at him thoughtfully and added, "If my calculations are correct, we destroyed or incapacitated about half of all the devices mounted in those racks. If we can accomplish that level in the target companies, the monetary impact will be huge."

"Yes, it will add up quickly for the Americans."

"It occurred to me that we should factor this into our calculations for how many robots we ship to each target site. In other words, if we could make a rough estimate of how many devices are at that location, we could determine how many robots to send. It would be a guess, but it might help us maximize the impact without wasting them on a small number of targets. No point sending hundreds of robots to attack a site with just a few computers."

"That's an excellent idea." She turned to Zhang Li. "Please work with Jiankang and Wei to make that happen. I think we are about ready to initiate our project. I would like you to implement these ideas by the end of the week. There's no reason to wait any longer."

"I will contact the General to seek his permission to begin, but I'm confident that he will be pleased with the success of our demonstration and will approve for us to start."

CHAPTER THIRTY-TWO

LATE-DECEMBER 2019

Manufacturing the drones was a delicate process, involving procuring x parts from a variety of sources and then assembling them in a clandestine factory. Mai and her team located a manufacturing facility, Pangolin Electronics Manufacturing Company, in the town of Jiangmen just southwest of Guangzhou. It was not a particularly large facility, but Mai judged that it was adequate for their purposes. Li Jun agreed, so they selected it and started setting up the necessary fabrication tools, assembly areas, shipping and packaging areas, warehouse rooms, and office areas to support the logistics personnel.

The office area was unremarkable, laid out and furnished like any other typical business, which was also true of the storage, packing, and shipping areas and warehouses. However, the assembly area was quite a sight to see. Along one long wall there were fifty 3D printers to be used to manufacture the simulated body parts, including the antennae, legs, head, thorax, and abdomen parts. The parts were printed from a reddish-brown plastic that was firm enough to work with but also flexible where necessary as in the antennae or hinges in the legs. The reddish-brown color resembled the color in actual cockroaches and was almost a perfect match. The head, thorax, and abdomen were printed as a single item to preserve the integrity of the body shape. On the bottom the body was left open so that the functional parts could be installed.

Functional parts were outsourced from surrounding small companies. This included the control circuit board, the tiny Lithium ion battery, the light and odor sensors, and the tiny piezo-electric actuators that drove the movements of the legs and would drive the needle into the acid container at the right time. Of course, the most dangerous part was the container for the fluoroantimonic acid which the team had concluded must be manufactured off-site for safety and delivered as a sealed, slightly pressurized PTFE (polytetrafluoroethylene) plastic container. The acid containers would be carefully inserted to the abdomen area late in the assembly process.

The light sensors were made of small delicate but sensitive photodiode arrays consisting of an array of independent light-detecting cells with a resolution of 200 by 300 pixels. They didn't provide a true image but were designed to tell the robot when a light source was nearby and to provide some direction and motion information to alert the robot of approaching dangers. They were installed on each side of the head in the same place as the eyes of a real cockroach, so they provided a stereoscopic view of the environment.

The sensors for odor detection were not small enough to fit into the antennae as in a real insect, so they were placed on the front of the head. It was important for them to be in a position where the robot cockroach could detect and avoid glue traps as quickly as possible. The control circuit board and uncharged Lithium ion battery were installed in the thorax. At full charge, the battery provided about two to four hours of operation depending on the level and type of activity of the robot. For safety and to prevent the robots from activating during shipping, the batteries would be charged wirelessly later. The wing coverlets containing the thin solar cells were attached to the dorsal thorax as well.

Miniaturized piezo-electric actuators were installed at the base of each leg and controlled the movement of the legs by causing the legs to bend back and forth. The choreography and coordination of these complex movements was driven by AI algorithms. Once all of the parts had been placed inside the robot's body, the assembly worker placed it onto a manufacturing test platform which completed the process by inserting test probes to make sure that it was wired correctly. The final step involved delicately heat-sealing the body along the ventral side. At that point, the robot cockroach was complete and ready to ship. Once it passed the quality control test step, it was ready to go.

The circuit boards, batteries, piezo-electric actuators, and light and odor sensors were manufactured off-site using automated and computerized techniques. However, the final assembly was a manual process done by approximately fifty Chinese workers. These workers were mostly young women who'd been recruited from rural areas and were a pretty inexpensive part of the overall costs. The workers were quite happy to have these jobs because it was more lucrative than working on the family farm. And even though the smarter ones might see through the explanation, they were perfectly willing to accept the story that they were making sophisticated toy robots. The real purpose was unknown to them, and of course, they didn't need to know.

Mai and Li calculated that they could reasonably assemble about four to six robots per day per worker, for a total production quantity of about 1,000 to 1,500 per week. They hoped that as the workers gained experience, the production levels might improve, but they could always add more workers later to ramp up.

After final assembly, the robots were delivered to the packaging department. There they were simply loaded into cardboard boxes holding exactly fifty robots. The boxes were labelled for shipping to another shell import company that Mai would set up in America.

Although initially they hadn't wanted any presence in America and they had planned to just ship the robots directly to the target sites, it became clear that they needed an intermediate step. They decided to set up a small false-front import company in Silicon Valley that would do several things: 1) act as the receiving point for all shipments; 2) repackage the robots as necessary; 3) charge the robots wirelessly; 4) activate the software with a Bluetooth connection; and 5) put shipping labels on the boxes and drop them off for local delivery.

This process had several advantages. It would prevent the robots from activating too early because they wouldn't be charged up and activated until they were placed in the final delivery box in America. It would be simpler as far as shipping because all shipments out of China would go to the same import company. They would have the flexibility to deliver the target site list to that company for last-minute labeling and local delivery via services like UPS or FedEx.

There was another benefit. Shipping dormant robots would permit them to get through customs more easily. They would easily pass customs scrutiny; they truly would appear to be harmless toys.

Mai recruited a few MSS agents in America to set up the shell import company and fine-tune the process. She would call the shell company Acme of China Toy Import Company.

CHAPTER THIRTY-THREE

INTERLUDE: THE NOVEL CORONAVIRUS, COVID-19 IN THE U.S AND AROUND THE WORLD.

The novel coronavirus (COVID-19) pandemic would have significant effects on the General's project, as well as the FBI investigation. From the outset of the investigation, Max's team was hindered by the lockdown rules that started in March 2020. They impacted the team's mobility, and some members of the team became infected so they had to quarantine, effectively removing them from the investigation. And for a while, Max's attention was diverted to investigating financial scams related to COVID-19.

The COVID-19 pandemic originated with an infected 55-year-old in the Hubei province of China on November 17, 2019. At first, COVID-19 was suspected to have started in so called "wet markets" where one can dine on fresh or recently killed exotic animals, a common practice in China. However, since many of the early cases appeared in people who had not eaten in wet markets, experts hypothesized that it may have jumped from bats to another animal and then to humans. Regardless of the origin, now the transmission moved directly from human to human.

As is typical for any pandemic, at first the numbers of infected individuals were modest. By December 15, the number of cases in China was 27; by December 20 the number of cases had risen to 60. By December 27 there were 180 cases. Unfortunately, there is a lot of evidence that points to active denial by the Chinese government with a steady stream of lies about the seriousness of the situation, and denials that human to human transmission was even possible. Healthcare professionals in China who publicly sounded the alarm were censored and in some cases jailed. The Chinese were on the leading edge of the COVID-19 pandemic which by March 13, 2020, had spread to 148,000 people globally and more than 81,000 in mainland China.

On January 6, 2020, the *New York Times* published its first report about the outbreak in Wuhan. While China continued to publicly suppress all information about the virus within China, the United States government was notified on January 3. Robert Redfield, the director of the CDC received initial reports about the emergence of a new coronavirus in Wuhan. Secretary Azar notified the National Security Council about the outbreak, and on January 6 the CDC issued a level-one travel watch for China's outbreak. The CDC also offered to send an investigative team to China to assist, but the offer was rejected.

In spite of the fact that there was clear evidence of COVID-19 passing among family members in China, the Chinese government continued to deny that the virus could spread among humans. On January 13, the first infected patient outside China was identified in Thailand: a 61-year-old visitor from Wuhan. On January 15, Japan reported its first case of COVID-19.

On January 7, the CDC and Department of Homeland Security's Customs and Border Protection announced that travelers from Wuhan to the United States would undergo entry screening for COVID-19 symptoms at the San Francisco, Los Angeles, and New York JFK airports.

On January 8, the HHS Secretary had his first discussion about COVID-19 with President Trump who was more interested in when flavored vaping products would be back on the market.

On January 21, the CDC announced the first case of COVID-19 in the United States, a Seattle resident who had returned from a trip to China six days earlier. By this point, millions of people had traveled from Wuhan carrying the virus all around China and the world. COVID-19 was now on the move in a deadly way. So when the General initiated his attacks in the Silicon Valley, the virus was just beginning to take hold.

PROJECT SABOTAGE

By January 23, Chinese authorities announced their first steps for a quarantine and lockdown of Wuhan. Of course, at this point since China was in the middle of their Lunar New Year, millions of Chinese citizens who were asymptomatic carriers were on the move. At this time, the chances of preventing a global outbreak had dwindled to zero, and the COVID-19 pandemic was well under way.

As far as the General's project was concerned, the Wuhan lockdown meant that the factory manufacturing the robot cockroaches was shut down for several months which prevented any deliveries to America for that time. It forced a roughly two-month gap in Mai's ability to mount attacks. Max and his team would see this as a pause in the attacks in America, but they had no understanding of the exact cause.

As of March 26, 2020, just over four months after the first case was observed in China, the COVID-19 virus had caused 466,955 cases and 21,162 deaths around the globe. And the numbers were continuing to rapidly rise. By June 2020, the COVID-19 pandemic had reached 8 million cases worldwide with more than 500,000 deaths. These numbers would continue to grow steadily and relentlessly. There seemed to be no end in sight.

PART IV

CHAPTER THIRTY-FOUR

APRIL 2020

Max was in his office reading through the latest stack of folders from his case trying to determine if he'd missed anything important, when he was startled by a call from Tom. About ten minutes later, he warily strolled into Tom's office, curious but not exactly enthusiastic about possibly getting additional work to do.

Sitting across from Tom after easing himself carefully into the chair to baby his back, he asked, "What's up, Tom?"

Tom noticed Max's pained expression but didn't comment on it. "The director's given us some new priorities, now that things are quiet for you."

Max was a bit annoyed both by Tom's dismissive attitude and his back pain. "What makes you think that things are quiet? I'm up to my eyeballs trying to solve the computer sabotage cases."

"You told me yourself that there was a pause in the attacks. Almost like a work stoppage."

Max felt a need to retreat. "Well, I did say that. But I think I also added that it was a mystery and it didn't necessarily mean that the attacks had stopped permanently. It may just be the calm before the storm. It seemed to correlate with our press release, but I find it hard to believe that the bad guys would suddenly stop because of that warning."

Tom couldn't resist a mild dig. "Maybe they heard that the famous FBI Agent Smart was closing in on them, and that scared them away?"

Max couldn't help but smile. "Funny. The attacks have slowed, and we haven't had any more calls. That tells me the criminals have paused their attacks, but I have no idea why. I fear they'll resume. Maybe they are just pausing so we drop our guard. I don't know."

"I'm not asking you to drop those cases, just put them on the back burner. Clearly, if they heat up again, you can jump right back on them."

"Fine. What's the new assignment?"

Tom pushed a printed page across his desk. "Have you seen this announcement from the Justice Department?"

"Sorry, I must have missed it. What does it say?"

"They notified federal prosecutors that anyone attempting to spread COVID-19 can be charged with terrorism. Threats or attempts to use the virus as a weapon will not be tolerated."

Max nodded. "That makes sense. After all, I'm sure COVID-19 fits the definition of a biological weapon."

"It certainly does, and individuals in a few states have already been charged for intentionally coughing on someone else."

"That's wonderful. Find yourself in prison for twenty years for being a complete asshole."

"Right." Tom rushed to his next point. "But the director wants to interpret this directive a bit more broadly. He wants us to be on the lookout for scammers trying to cash in on the public fears by spreading false information, especially bogus claims like free home-test kits, protective equipment for sale, or miracle cures. Some of these are just variations of phishing scams or click-bait. But other scams, particularly the miracle cure offers, are downright dangerous. In some instances, people have ingested cures that actually made them worse, and in a few cases actually killed them."

Max had seen this before. "The motto of many skilled scammers is to never let a perfectly good crisis go to waste."

Tom had seen a lot throughout his career. "That's for sure. And they have no qualms about preying on the most vulnerable. They rely on tried-and-true tricks only changing the name on the scam. This COVID-19 situation is so huge that it will be a gold mine for scammers of all types."

"You bet. For one thing, so many people are working at home that they could be highly vulnerable by not having the same security they had in the office. People are worried and distracted; they need support and will be more susceptible to offers that sound legitimate. And with the amount of money that Congress is planning to inject into the economy... the pigs will be lining up at the trough."

"This one is going to be a tsunami of scams from con artists."

"Absolutely, so what do you want me to do?"

"I want you to identify any obvious local COVID-19 scams. It shouldn't be too difficult."

"I'll have Jason and Monica work on this as well. They're both spending a lot of time on their laptops already, working remotely."

"As soon as you uncover any scams, let's jump on them. The public is on edge, and it would be good to have some success stories to let them know we're watching out for their interests."

"Okay, I'll get started right now."

"By the way, how are you holding up? And your team?"

Max had to think about his response. "I think I'm doing okay. So far, I haven't gotten any symptoms, and I don't think I've been exposed. Hopefully, that won't happen, but who knows?"

Then Max thought he should update Tom on another problem. "Unfortunately, my back surgery has been postponed indefinitely because the hospital is saving their capacity to treat potential COVID-19 patients. They can't tell me when I can expect to get it done."

Tom acknowledged with a sympathetic nod. "Sorry to hear that. I know that you were looking forward to a fix for your back pain."

"And how about Jason and Monica?"

"Jason's worried about his parents. He isn't wearing it on his sleeve, but I can tell that he's very concerned. He can't even visit them. He's pretty depressed about it, since all he can do is stand outside and wave through the window while on the phone." Max continued, "And Monica's stuck at home taking care of her kids since the schools closed. Both are still productive working from home, but it has certainly added to everyone's stress and it's beginning to interfere with some of the investigations. For example, we may have to do a lot of our interviews with Zoom or Facetime. Hopefully, this lock-down ends soon."

Tom let that sink in. "Well, I'm no expert on pandemics, but I doubt it will. I'm hearing rumors that the lockdown may last until June or later. Just saying."

"You're probably right. Let me get started." Max strolled back to his office after grabbing a fresh cup of coffee from the breakroom. In terms of scams, Max was not an expert, but you can't live in America without being exposed to scams on a daily basis. They run the gamut from scams designed to steal your personal information, to scams trying to pry money from your wallet. The most nefarious could harm physical health. Miracle medications or supposed cures for COVID-19 were the latest versions of the old snake-oil pitch. The World Health Organization identified at least a dozen myths about cures. Even silly coronavirus cure-all claims can be dangerous when they deceive people into believing they are protected. And in one case, the situation turned fatal. A couple in Arizona believed the rumors that Hydroxychloroquine was a game changer for treatment and prevention of COVID-19, so they drank some in the form of a fish tank disinfectant. She ended up in critical care, and he died. The Internet sounding board is clearly not the resource you turn to for medical advice.

It didn't take Max long to find a scam to focus on. The scam artist's name was Ephron Mendelson, probably a false name, and he conveniently listed an email address. His pitch was a version of the classic get-rich-quick scheme. Ephron was soliciting investors in a pill that could prevent a person from catching COVID-19, or to cure infections. According to Ephron, this was the "money-making opportunity of a lifetime, better than investing in Apple at the beginning." He promised that a $300,000 investment would yield a return of $30 million.

How could you pass on that? Max thought with a sarcastic chuckle.

Ephron's company was called COVID-19 Prevention Solutions, Inc., and claimed to have two former Los Angeles Lakers on its board of directors. In an Instagram video, viewed over a million times, Ephron claimed that if he "took the pill and walked through a New York City hospital filled with COVID-19 patients," he would not contract the virus.

This is a particularly cruel scam. When many people are suffering and losing loved ones, the last thing we need is a con artist hawking a miracle cure that he knows is not tested, guaranteed, nor approved, thought Max.

So, he contacted Ephron with the intention of setting up a sting.

CHAPTER THIRTY-FIVE

Max sent Ephron an urgent email explaining that he was desperate to find a cure for his ailing parents and that since they were already infected, time was critical. He provided his cellphone number and waited for the call.

Ephron called back about three hours later, apparently eager to fleece another sucker. "Sorry I was a bit slow getting back to you. As you can imagine, I'm busy these days. Please describe your situation. I need to know if this investment is right for you."

"Well, Ephron—is it okay if I call you Ephron?"

"Certainly. Is it okay for me to call you Max?" Con artists like to convince their victims that they're your friend in order to gain your trust.

"Yes," said Max as he cringed. "Here's my situation—both of my parents have tested positive for the virus, and while they haven't been hospitalized, they feel sick and are scared out of their wits. I saw your information on the web, and I'd really like to buy your cure for the virus. Also, since I am being exposed on a daily basis when I visit them, I want to invest in your preventative medicine for myself so that I don't get it. So, how can I buy in?"

"Well, first let me ask how much you're willing to invest?"

Max hesitated just long enough to give Ephron the impression that he wasn't sure how to proceed. "I saw on your website that a $300,000 investment is guaranteed to return $3 million. I don't have that kind of money."

Ephron tried to comfort Max. "Don't be put off by that. That was just an example of what investors can expect to earn in the future. Rest assured it does not mean that $300,000 is the minimum requirement. So, let me ask you again, how much are you able to invest?"

Max wanted to string him along a bit by making his story sound more dire. "First, let me make it clear that I'm not doing this to make money, though that would certainly be nice. I want to save my parents. My investments have taken a hit with the market, so I was thinking I could invest about $50,000. Would that be enough to provide me with a cure for two people, and also the preventative treatment?"

Max could almost hear Ephron drooling on the other end of the call. Ephron replied, "Yes. That would work. I'm selling shares for $1,000 per share, which would give you fifty shares. But you need to act quickly. My supply is limited because sales have been brisk and we are just ramping up production. Also, as the word gets out, the price per share will go up so I can't guarantee it will always be this low. Clearly your need is also immediate, so there is no reason to wait."

Another technique used by con artists is to create a sense of urgency. You want the sucker to act immediately so they don't have time for second thoughts. Also, it helps to put a relatively high price on things. It's human nature that if the price is too low, people get suspicious.

Max exclaimed with an audible sigh of relief, "Wow. That's great. I was afraid I might not be able to buy enough."

"Absolutely."

Max responded with an appropriate mix of eagerness and desperation in his voice. "Okay, I really need this medication. I can arrange with my bank this afternoon to get a certified check and then meet you somewhere to close the deal. Will that work?"

"Yes. But you could also just do a wire transfer if that would be more convenient."

Max knew it was important for the sting to collect physical evidence. "That might be more convenient, but I have to admit I'm more comfortable doing it the old-fashioned way. I'm kind of a luddite. I can barely manage email and my iPhone. So, I'd prefer to meet in person. Perhaps you can bring the paperwork for the investment and I'll sign it on the spot."

"Okay. I understand. Where would you like to meet?"

"How about the entrance to the Moscone Center? Three o'clock?"

"That's fine. How will I recognize you?"

Max looked up trying to decide how to describe himself. "Look for a tall guy with graying hair, about fifty years old, walking slowly, wearing a dark blue face mask. I have a bad back, so I walk kind of awkwardly. I'll wear a dark blue sport coat and khaki slacks."

Ephron simply responded. "I'll see you at three."

CHAPTER THIRTY-SIX

Max would have several more agents nearby but out of sight to assist with the sting in case the suspect tried to flee. Max wasn't kidding about his bad back and his days of chasing down criminals were long gone.

His secretary made a trip to the bank to get a certified check. It was important for Ephron to physically hand him some product and to accept the check as payment. The physical exchange for a deal was critical evidence. He would wear a wire and record with his iPhone in his coat pocket. That way he'd have two sets of audio evidence. Also, he'd have one of the agents film the exchange from a distance.

Max showed up at the Convention Center in downtown San Francisco right on time, 3:00 p.m. Usually just referred to as the Moscone Center, it is the largest convention center in the city. Located on Howard Street, it occupies two whole city blocks. Max walked up to one of the glass door entrances and looked up and down the block. Because of the stay-at-home order, the sidewalk in front of the modern glass façade was eerily deserted.

A middle-aged man with gray hair walked toward him. While he was dressed in a fitted business suit, his appearance was nondescript. He was neither good-looking nor ugly—just rather plain. A person you might walk by without noticing because he had no attention-drawing features. But the timing and location suggested that he must be Ephron. After all, there was no one else on the entire stretch of sidewalk in front of the building.

"Ephron, is that you?"

"Yes, and of course you must be Max."

"Yes, that's me. Thanks for agreeing to meet. I can't wait to get this cure to my parents."

"Well, we'll make that happen. Did you bring the check?"

"Yes, I did. Did you bring the paperwork and the medicine?"

"I have both."

Max pointed to one of the long concrete benches along the glass façade and indicated that he'd like to sit down. Then he decided to make Ephron a bit uncomfortable. "I see you aren't wearing a face mask, so why don't we sit on opposite ends of this bench and use it to exchange things?"

Ephron sighed with a touch of disgust indicating that he didn't agree with the face mask rules. Nevertheless, he took a seat at the far end of the bench.

Ephron put the documents on the bench and pushed them to Max. Max took a few minutes to read the paperwork to ensure it provided the evidence he needed, then signed and slid it back to Ephron with the check. Ephron then sent a small envelope across the bench to Max. Max opened it and pulled out two small vials each labeled *COVID-19 Formulation*. And after looking them over, he asked, "These are the pills that will cure my parents? There are only about a dozen in each vial. Is that enough?"

Ephron smiled proudly. "Yes, these pills are the cure. They should take them twice a day for three days and that will eliminate the virus from their bodies."

Max frowned. "But how will I know they've been cured?"

Ephron responded confidently. "That's simple. After they take the cure for three days, have them tested for COVID-19, and you will find that they test negative. And the good news is that after they're cured, the medication will prevent them from being reinfected, so it's doubly effective. It's a cure and a vaccine."

Max shook his head from side to side and acted amazed. "Is it guaranteed to work?"

Ephron nodded vigorously. "Absolutely. We worked hard on developing this medicine, and it is *guaranteed* to work as advertised."

Max smiled to indicate he was satisfied with Ephron's answer. "Well, that's wonderful. I really enjoyed doing business with you. Now, please look to your right and smile. You're on candid camera."

Ephron glanced from side to side with a mixture of bewilderment and surprise. "What are you talking about?"

"It's simple, Ephron. I'm FBI Special Agent Max Smart, and I'm arresting you for felony fraud. You have your rights, and I will read them to you now."

Ephron's face drained of color, and he looked like he might get sick on the spot. Ephron noticed for the first time that three young men had quietly approached from opposite directions and were less than fifty feet away. He assumed from their dress and demeanor that they were FBI agents, so he made no attempt to flee. One of them stepped behind him and handcuffed him, and they began escorting him to their car at the end of the block.

Max was surprised at how easy it had been to nab this guy. He was either too stupid or too full of himself to realize that the meeting might be a setup. Or perhaps Ephron thought that the COVID-19 crisis was so bad that agencies like the FBI would be too busy to be on the lookout for scammers like him. He might have assumed he could just fly under the radar for a while, bilk a bunch of investors, then hit the road. Strike while the iron was hot, then skip town.

What Ephron didn't realize was that the government was incented to stop these kinds of scams and misinformation before they became too widespread. The government needed to "flatten the curve" on scams in a similar way that they were trying to flatten the curve on the spread of COVID-19 itself. The evidence they had collected would be enough to put Ephron away for quite a long stretch.

PART V

CHAPTER THIRTY-SEVEN

JANUARY 2020

O nce manufacturing was underway, Mai recruited two agents in America to set up a local import company. They were both U.S. citizens, recruited by MSS several years ago. They had never been asked to perform any duties. They were "sleeper" agents, perfect for this assignment.

John Chen was raised in Palo Alto. His parents had emigrated to America in response to the Chinese Communist takeover of Hong Kong. They were well-to-do and wished to get out of China fearing that their wealth was about to be taken away. John grew up thinking of himself as a normal American. He was a graduate of the business school at Stanford University with a strong work ethic. However, his parents also instilled in him a split and confusing mix of loyalties. While he was a U.S. citizen, he also harbored hidden loyalties to his ancestral country of China. And like a lot of young people he was still somewhat naïve. And perhaps he had played too many video games which gave him the impression that life was also a game, so when Mai approached him her proposal seemed like a lark or adventure. He certainly didn't think it through carefully. And, with the COVID-19 pandemic ramping up, he had been laid off with dim prospects. Therefore, the money that Mai dangled in front of him was a major factor in his decision to work for her.

Debbie Wong had recently dropped out of San Jose State University. She was partway through the nursing program when she came to the conclusion that she wasn't cut out to take care of sick people. And the COVID-19 crisis had confirmed her decision to not pursue a nursing career, but she didn't have any idea what she wanted to do next. Now in her early twenties, she was naïve and inexperienced, and also in need of income. Jobs were difficult to find. So she jumped on Mai's offer to work on a project that sounded harmless enough. At least on the surface.

Mai sent John an encrypted email outlining her requirements. She described the project in general terms, only giving him highlights and made it was clear that she wanted him to move ahead as rapidly as he could.

John located a small site in a light industrial complex area of the city of East Palo Alto. He signed a lease using the name Acme of China Toy Import Company, LLC, after explaining to the owner that he planned to import a variety of toys from China. The landlord was happy to have John as a new tenant. The building was located on Demeter Street in the middle of a collection of one-story small businesses, including plumbing, woodworking, fabricating services, and auto repair. These light industrial areas are scattered throughout the Silicon Valley. John picked this location for its convenient access to local transportation to deliver packages from his office to the target locations.

John purchased a couple heavy-duty wireless chargers from a local electronics distributor. All that was required to charge the robots was to place the box on top of the flat charger. When Mai sent him the PC application to activate the robots with a Bluetooth connection, he installed it on a laptop computer. It was pretty straightforward—all he had to do was place a box of robots next to the laptop, the app would report how many robots were inside, and then after clicking on the button labeled *Activate*, it would report back after a few minutes how many of the robots inside were successfully activated. Normally that would be all fifty. He needed to find out from Mai what to do if the number didn't match. He assumed it would be problematic to send out any robots that were not fully powered and activated.

John explained carefully to Debbie, "What we need to do is pretty easy. We will receive about thirty boxes a week at the outset, and then may ramp up later. Each box will contain fifty robot cockroaches in a dormant state. In many cases, we can just plan on shipping the box directly to a target by printing and attaching a new address label. But before we can send it, the robots must be activated. All you need to do is place the unopened box on top of a charger for a couple hours. The next step is to place the box next to the laptop and use the app to activate it. Once that's done, the box is ready to go. I think the best approach is for one of us to take it directly to UPS, FedEx, or the USPS. I thought about having UPS just pick them up here, but that might draw too much attention. The neighbors might find it odd to see so many pickups out back."

"That's all there is to the job? Sounds too easy."

"It does, doesn't it? Mai will expect us to be thorough. We can't make any mistakes, like mislabeling boxes, for example."

"That shouldn't be a problem, considering the low volume of shipments per week."

"That's true. There's one twist though."

"What's that?"

"See those larger boxes over there?" John pointed to a stack of folded cardboard boxes in the corner of the store-room. They were printed on the outside with the logo and product description of a leading computer server provider. "For some of the target sites, we will repackage the robots into those boxes, putting two hundred in each. Then they get the same treatment. New printed shipping labels, battery charging followed by activation, then drop off at a local ship-ping service."

"Why the repackaging into those boxes?"

"My understanding is that it's part of the plan to sneak them past security. I think the idea is that they'll be delivered to data centers before they are opened. The boxes will be inside the secured area before they know about the robots in the box. At least, I think that's the purpose."

Debbie was impressed. "Pretty sneaky."

John simply added, "At any rate, regardless of the reason, we just need to do it whenever Mai directs us to. She will send us target lists that will tell us what to do."

"When do we expect the first shipments to arrive?"

"Next week."

"I can't wait. This should be fun."

As promised, the first shipment of robots came the following week. It consisted of thirty small cardboard boxes that John Chen assumed held fifty robots each. The total was 1,500 to be sent to eleven companies.

His first target list included Alligator Enterprises and nine other small technology companies, and one large company, Gigabit Networking Corporation. The first set of ten companies would be easy, only requiring printing and attaching new labels, then powering and activating them. The boxes would remain sealed.

John took twenty boxes and opened them so he could move the robot cockroaches into the larger faux-labeled cartons for delivery to ten different buildings at Gigabit. He placed a hundred robots in each carton and carefully sealed them shut with Mylar tape so that no light could get inside . He placed them onto the charger and activated them with the Bluetooth app.

John was a detail-oriented person, sort of a compulsive type. "I'm going to organize our workflow to avoid accidentally releasing activated robots into our own office. I don't want to risk opening one of your boxes by mistake after you've activated it. What do you think?"

Debbie brightened up a bit. "I hadn't thought about that, but you are right."

He asked her to print the labels and take care of activating all of the remaining boxes to ready them for local delivery.

When they had finished preparing the boxes, he said, "Debbie, please drop off your packages at UPS. I'll take these larger ones to a couple of other UPS drop sites."

"Here we go. Keep your fingers crossed."

"It's nice to finally get started. We are supposed to get another shipment from China in the next few days, and then at least one shipment per week after that."

CHAPTER THIRTY-EIGHT

After Mai sat down across from the General, he looked up at her with a slight smile on his face. "Mai, it's clear that the attacks have been successful."

Mai was pleased, so she brightened up and smiled back cheerfully. "Yes, General. We've attacked over two hundred companies. As you know, there was a two-month pause while our production facilities were locked down for the virus. But the factory has been able to resume production, and so we can resume attacks right away."

The General frowned and then gave her a serious stare. "I'm pleased with your progress, though I've been disappointed by the work stoppages in Hubei Province that have disrupted our project. Now I think it's time to put more pressure on the Americans. They 'll undoubtedly figure out what's going on at some point, and before that happens, I wish to inflict as much damage as possible."

Mai was aware that the work stoppages had interrupted their project but unsure how to respond. "What precisely would you like me to do?"

The General looked at her as if the answer was obvious. "It's quite simple. I want you to shift your focus from companies to large data centers."

Mai couldn't quite resist involuntarily shaking her head slightly in in objection, "You realize that those are secure facilities and will be much harder to penetrate than smaller companies?"

The General dismissed her with a wave of his hand. "Of course, I know that," he said. "Disabling a major data center would create widespread damage. The data centers host support services for a large customer base, so crippling one would harm many customers, not just the data center itself."

Mai smiled. "I suppose that's true. I don't know a lot about data centers."

The General was happy to teach her. "Data centers rent computing power out to a company, host their business applications, including websites, shipping, billing, and so forth. The small business saves money because they don't have to build and maintain their own systems. And the data center manages the systems and ensures their operation. If you knock out the servers, well..."

"Clearly that would have a major impact."

"So, tell me how you can do it."

Mai responded after a short hesitation. "We concluded earlier that the only way would be to bribe insiders."

The General nodded. "That makes sense, considering how secure data centers are."

Mai continued to explain her approach. "I'll have Zhang Li review the data she has been building about identifying co-operating Americans, and cross-reference that to identify who works at a data center."

"Do you have assets in America who could do the recruiting?"

Mai realized it was time for her shell import company to do double duty. "Yes, I have two individuals already there, handling the local processing of robots. One of them, John Chen, is the best bet for this job."

The General didn't wish to dwell on this topic. "Do what you think is necessary. What would you use to recruit them?"

Mai thought the answer was obvious but offered a response. "I assume we'd rely on the normal techniques—bribes, blackmail."

"Sounds good. I'll let you work out the details with your team."

"I was also thinking that we would need to use more cockroaches for a single data center attack. We'll need to wait until we have enough robots to launch the attacks."

"Use as many as necessary. I'll leave that to your team's judgement. Expending thousands of robots on a single data center will be worth it."

"Okay. I'll get my team moving on this."

CHAPTER THIRTY-NINE

MARCH 2020

Back in her office, Mai asked Zhang Li to search for employee matches for three data centers in the San Francisco area: BizMoat Data Hosting Solutions in South San Francisco, Bulwark and Megaladon Data Services in Emeryville, and Leatherback Data Vault Corporation in San Mateo. She selected them because of their locations as well as their size.

Zhang Li identified potential conspirators at each data center by finding their vulnerabilities based on the hacked Equifax information. The information was a bit dated but provided a view into their situations and she assumed their behavior had stayed consistent.

Vincent Agassizi worked at BizMoat Data Hosting Solutions. He was 45 and had worked there for about eight years as a computer maintenance engineer. Unfortunately, Vincent had a gambling problem, which was unknown to his company, but a terrible burden for him. Vincent loved to take the short, one-hour flights to Las Vegas, where he often racked up sizable losses, especially at the sports gambling venues. It was reflected in his lateness paying his bills, and he was consistently behind on payments, particularly on credit cards which had steadily increasing balances. He managed to make the minimum payments, which of course the credit card companies loved. Vincent's debts were steadily mounting up.

Alton Murphy had worked at Bulwark and Megalodon Data Services since he graduated from college six years earlier. Alton was an application engineer helping customers set up their business services, and he was considered to be a talented software designer. His problem was that his student loan debt was staggering, close to $200,000. In order to get through college, he had been forced to take out loans. And, he had not been good about tracking how fast they were accumulating. Now he despaired, worrying that he would never pay them off because the principle balance just kept increasing.

Janice Chaudry-Jones, an employee at Leatherback Data Vault Corporation LLC, was in her mid-thirties and had been working in information technology her entire career. She had met her ex-husband at a previous job, and after an ugly divorce, she was saddled with large debts, mainly lawyer fees. She had two young children, and her husband had left California and refused to pay child support. Making ends meet every month was a significant challenge.

Each of them was contacted separately; there was no need for them to meet each other. John Chen conveyed the same offer to each individual. The cover story was that they'd be paid handsomely to place boxes inside the data center that were capable of wirelessly skimming information from the surrounding equipment. It was explained to them that even though the boxes were labeled as computer equipment from a legitimate company, they actually contained top-secret wireless technology from China. No effort was made to hide the fact that this was a Chinese espionage project. It was assumed that they might only go along with this cover story if the purpose of the boxes appeared to be relatively harmless. Even though stealing data was far from a harmless activity, it might be perceived as more acceptable, making it likely that they'd accept the bribes.

Janice had asked what would happen if the secret technology was discovered, and she was informed that if the devices were discovered, any attempt to open them or tamper with them would cause the devices to self-destruct. She was also told that the devices did not have any traceable information on them—that is, no brand names or serial numbers, nor any indication of where they were made. John worked hard to convince her that the devices could never be traced back to her. She agreed to go along with the scheme.

Vincent and Alton were uncomfortable with the idea of helping the Chinese, thinking it would mean they were traitors. However, they were both desperate for money, so they finally swallowed their objections and agreed to do it, assuming that they would not be caught.

When they asked what they would have to do and when, the answer was simply: "You only need to use your official access to put these boxes inside the computer center. Once you have done so, you can just leave the room. No further action is required."

PART VI

CHAPTER FORTY

APRIL 2020

John was told to prepare for the large data center attacks. He postponed smaller attacks to make sure he had enough robots. The team had estimated that he should prepare about 5,000 robots for each attack, so he had to wait several weeks until he had enough.

His ability to accumulate enough robots had been impacted by the two-month factory shutdowns in China caused by the pandemic. During that time, he had received none, and now that manufacturing had resumed, he would need to stall for a number of weeks. Considering he was receiving about 1,500 per week, he would need about ten weeks to meet his needs. So, the pause in attacks observed by Tom and Max was the result of these combined factors.

John had spent some of the break building and testing special boxes with automatic flaps he needed for the data center attacks. He decided to build them himself for security reasons, and the design was fairly simple. Small flaps were cut into one end of the box, and then a hinged actuator mechanism was installed that could be triggered by a timer circuit. The bugs would lay dormant in the box until the flap opened, then when their own internal clocks reached the appointed time that night, they would leave the box.

John arranged with Vincent, Alton, and Janice, his three conspirators, to expect deliveries to their sites addressed directly to them. John explained that the boxes would be labeled as normal replacement servers with a well-known name printed on the outside.

Each of the conspirators was quite surprised that John was sending them four boxes, not just one as he had described in their first meeting.

John responded with an offhand explanation. "Sorry about the change of plans. You'll be shipped four boxes. It doesn't change anything about your tasks." It was presented as a done deal, so none of them pushed back. Too late anyway—they'd already received an advance partial payment.

The attacks were scheduled for the following week. All three were to happen the same night in the same way.

Janice Chaudry-Jones at Leatherback Data Vault Corporation retrieved the four cartons addressed to her from the shipping department. She placed them on a dolly and wheeled them down the hallway to the secure area of the data center containing the long rows of racks. Using her access badge, she entered the secure area and rolled the dolly into the huge room at the heart of the data center and placed the dolly and boxes unobtrusively on one side of the room. Then she promptly exited. Her entry and exit had been noted by guards watching security cameras, but her activities seemed routine. Her task was complete, and she was nervous to leave the room. She thought maybe she should just leave work entirely, claim a sudden illness or some other excuse, and go home. Sounded like a great idea.

What Janice didn't know, of course, was that absolute mayhem was going to erupt later that night.

At about 3:00 a.m., the panels on the four boxes popped open. Almost simultaneously, the bugs started streaming out. The data center was their perfect environment, and they wasted no time scattering throughout the facility, crawling into the racks, over and under the equipment, and into the spaces under the raised flooring. In a short time, 5,000 robot cockroaches had infested the data center like a tidal wave flooding onto an exposed coastline. And like a tidal wave, the destruction would be terrible.

The robot cockroaches attacked all the various targets they'd been programmed to seek out—servers, routers, Ethernet switches, power cords, and network cables. As in other attacks, once the robots started, it didn't take long for them to finish—only about sixty minutes. By that time, the robots had destroyed 2,700 servers, 180 routers, fifty-three Ethernet switches, and innumerable cables and power cords.

The same events played out at the other two data centers with similar results.

Because data centers are designed with numerous reliability and failsafe features, some of the damage was more limited than it appeared. Data centers rely on the principle of redundancy to maximize survivability and resilience. Redundancy simply means that critical components are duplicated so that failure of one component does not cause the entire system to fail.

Redundancy begins in the individual hardware. For example, servers typically have two or more fans for cooling and failure of one fan is not critical. Likewise, other internal components such as hard drives and power supplies are usually redundant as well. Redundancy also extends to Ethernet switches and routers and the connections between them.

Software programs are also duplicated on two or more servers. In the case of the BizMoat Data Hosting Solutions attack, larger customers were hosted on numerous servers across the data center facility, but that was not true for the smallest customers. Many small customers suffered from a total loss of their Internet websites, ordering and billing, shipping and delivery, accounting, or other critical business applications. So, they were totally knocked out of business. Often, damage to the company's reputation was the most significant loss.

The systems of the three attacked data centers were designed to the industry standard of "five nines" reliability, meaning 99.999% uptime, or less than 5.38 minutes of outages over an entire year. Under normal operating conditions, they could guarantee this goal. However, none of the data centers could have imagined that they would suffer this type of bizarre attack which could cause such widespread failure. The data centers were designed to withstand storms, power outages, floods, fires, and earthquakes. They had implemented comprehensive security technology and sufficient security personnel to ward off intrusions. They monitored the health of the equipment, tracking data center temperature, equipment overheating, and equipment component failures.

All of these features mitigated the attacks to some extent but could not stop the extensive havoc wrought by the robot cockroaches. They may as well have been hit by a tsunami.

Larger hosted customers were not completely knocked out of service because their applications were hosted on a large number of servers. However, they were forced to operate at reduced capacity, in which case the slowness of their services would create unhappy customers.

Overall, the attacks were a nightmare for the data center personnel, creating a huge amount of work to replace and rebuild the hosted services. It would take time to fully recover.

Many small companies were already living on the edge because of the business drought caused by the COVID-19 pandemic and might never recover.

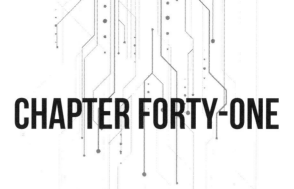

CHAPTER FORTY-ONE

The data center security team at Leatherback Data Vault Corporation were the first to piece together a series of odd events at their facility. Their video surveillance system had recorded images of IT technician Janice Chaudry-Jones delivering four boxes to the secure server area. She had explained to the security guard that they contained replacement servers that were to be installed the following day. After she left the room, the boxes just sat in a stack on a dolly off to the side.

That night at about three in the morning, a series of strange things occurred. The boxes appeared to pop open on the sides, followed by numerous objects streaming onto the floor, then scurrying in all directions. The image was not clear enough for the security team to figure out what they were seeing, but for all intents and purposes, they could have sworn that they were watching insects running around. In some views, it appeared the bugs were crawling onto the racks of equipment, or up cables, and distributing themselves throughout the data center. It was an odd sight.

Within no more than thirty minutes, NOC alarms were lighting up showing numerous failures, including power outages, link failures, CPU failures, disk drive failures, and fan failures. The number of alarms steadily increased, and the wall-mounted monitors flashed with warning indicators. The NOC engineers couldn't see the attacks, but it was clear to all of them that something was drastically wrong. Two of them, Randy Bates and Stan Silver, ran to the server room to see what was going on, but as soon as they opened the door, they were assaulted by painful, noxious fumes. After just two minutes, both engineers left the room because the irritation in their eyes, throats, and lungs was overwhelming. Unbeknownst to them at the time, the ceiling fans had kicked into high gear and were valiantly attempting to suck out the contaminated air. Also, the halon fire suppression system was about to go off, but hadn't yet because the fans were effective enough. The system recognized that there were no heat spots, so it ruled out a fire. That was fortunate because if the fire suppression system had gone off, it would have added to the damage.

This sequence of events was presented to Max Smart the next day by company executives who had called the FBI to report the incident.

Max had been told by Tom that there had been three attacks on separate data centers in the past twenty-four hours and that he had to add them to his investigation immediately. Max chose to meet with Leatherback Data Vault Corporation, and he asked Monica to meet with BizMoat and Jason to meet with Bulwark and Megaladon Services. Obviously, the situation had gotten more serious, and he thought it would be most efficient to conduct simultaneous interviews.

Max was joined in a conference room at Leatherback Data Vault Corporation by Howard Fiennes, CEO, Sanjay Srinivasen, CTO, and Larry Mierson, Director of Security. They were sitting far apart around the large table and everyone was wearing a face mask, including Max.

He quickly launched the discussion. "I've reviewed the information provided by Larry, and I'm pleased to tell you that you may have provided our first solid clues. The attack on your data center follows a pattern that we've seen in over a hundred local companies. It seems that an infestation of cockroaches is introduced into the building, followed by some sort of attack on the equipment. We were beginning to think that the two were related, but as you can imagine, no one could understand how cockroaches could damage computers."

Larry immediately jumped in angrily. "You've seen these attacks before? Why weren't we warned? That seems negligent to me."

Max didn't take the bait and calmly responded, "I don't think negligence is a fair conclusion. By the way, we did send out an official press release warning all local companies about these unusual attacks. I guess you didn't see it. But let's not get off on the wrong foot here. We're here to help."

As Director of Security, it was his responsibility to stay informed about FBI alerts. Larry backed off sheepishly. "Sorry. As you can imagine, we're all quite upset."

Max was happy to have defused the situation, so he pressed on. "Okay, I absolutely understand. Please know that the FBI is also frustrated, and we are working to solve these cases. As I said, I think that your incident may provide us with the first really solid clues."

Howard finally spoke up. "In addition to what you've been told by Larry, what else do you need to know?"

"Mainly, I need some clarifications. I understand that a large number of insects swarmed out of the four boxes and that you have this on videotape. Are the four boxes still there? Where are the insects now? Is there any evidence of their presence? Can you provide me with an inventory of the damaged equipment along with cost estimates of the damage?"

Howard nodded, acknowledging the questions. "That's a lot of questions, but I'll take a stab at it. Yes, if you look at the video, you can see the insects swarming out of the boxes, emerging from the openings on the sides. After the incident finished—that is, after all the damage had been done—we didn't see any further evidence of their existence. None to be found anywhere we looked. Vanished, apparently. The most obvious signs of damage were small holes in the front sides of the equipment—small, round holes that looked like something had corroded the ventilation screens. Also, many cables were eaten through with portions of them literally dissolved or melted. Inside some of the equipment, we also found corrosion on circuit boards."

"That's consistent with what we have seen in other attacks."

Howard seemed a bit put off by Max's comment. "Thanks for the feedback, but it's not particularly comforting. The boxes are still in the data center. Do you want to see them?"

Max knew that would be helpful. "Yes, once we finish here, I'd like a tour of the damaged area."

Howard added, "Certainly. As far as an inventory, we are still compiling that. It will take time. The damage is quite extensive." Howard stood in an attempt to move the meeting along, "Unless there's something else you want to discuss, why don't we go down to the data center so you can see the crime scene yourself?"

Max still had questions, so he remained seated and asked, "There are just a few more clarifications that I need. First, did you notice anything else unusual about the attacks? Or did you see anything odd afterwards?"

Howard sat back down, but Sanjay took over at this point. "As a matter of fact, a couple odd things happened. First, there was smoke or mist coming out of some of the equipment. It dissipated fairly quickly because the overhead cooling fans sucked it out. However, when we tried to enter the room, there were fumes which were painful, so we had to wait for the fans to vent the area. It took several hours. But the air in there still seems caustic, and it burns your eyes if you stay very long. Two maintenance technicians were taken to the emergency room because they were complaining about chest pains in addition to eye and throat irritation."

Max made a note of this new information. "Anything else?"

Sanjay continued. "Yes. Another odd thing was that there were little globs or piles of residue on the floor. They were not identifiable. We cleaned them up with wet mops."

Max jotted down some additional notes in his notebook. "Okay. Let's go down to the data center."

When they got into the secured area, Max was assaulted by the fumes. As they had said, it was somewhat painful. The four cardboard boxes were off to the side, with the open flaps clearly visible. Max had them open up one box, and it was completely empty with the exception of a small hinged mechanical device on the flap. He had them open up the other three, and they were empty as well with the same attached hinge.

"I will have these taken to our forensics team so they can analyze them for evidence."

Max walked over to the closest computer rack, so he could examine the damage to the servers. It was consistent with the damage he had seen at other companies.

"I've also requested that a local forensics team come here . I'm particularly interested in having them analyze these damaged areas to confirm what chemicals were involved. Now let's get out of here. This atmosphere is just too uncomfortable."

CHAPTER FORTY-TWO

R andy Bates had worked as a maintenance technician at Leatherback Data Vault Corporation for about two years. From a young age, he was considered to be sort of a computer geek, so this job was a perfect fit. He was not as comfortable around people as he was around computers, and he actually enjoyed the long hours in the data center. His job involved everything from installing computer applications or software patches to load-balancing customer services and re-placing equipment. There was plenty of work and usually the time passed swiftly. But not necessarily smoothly. The night of the attacks, he was sent to the equipment room to find out what had caused so many alarms. Something was seriously wrong. He was accompanied by another maintenance techni-cian, Stan Silvers.

Stan was a computer nerd like Randy. They'd become good friends. They shared a love for technology and could spend hours talking about hardware and software, applica-tions, network design, and any number of arcane subjects. It was not unusual for them to help each other out. And in this case, the alarms were so numerous and serious that it would be especially useful for both of them to check out the problem.

When they had entered the equipment room during the attack, both immediately noticed the acrid odor which assaulted their sense of smell and irritated their eyes. At first, they tried to dismiss it because the problems in the data center were so important that they felt the need to get inside and start to work on the solution. Unfortunately, after just a few minutes, they couldn't tolerate the atmosphere. The irritation in their eyes, tightness in their throats, and pain in their lungs was becoming overwhelming. They left the room and walked down a long hallway to the break room to rinse their eyes and get something cold to drink. In Randy's case especially, the pain in his chest was awful—so bad that he wondered if he was having a heart attack caused by the sudden stressful situation.

Stan called Larry Mierson, Director of Security, and explained the situation. Larry came to the break room to check on them, and he was absolutely appalled when he entered the room and saw Randy and Stan sitting at the table looking wan and miserable. They both appeared to be in considerable pain and were hunched over leaning on the table clutching their chests.

"You guys look like shit," was all Larry could say.

Stan rolled his eyes and winced from the pain in his chest and throat. "No kidding. I think I might be having a heart attack."

Larry was sympathetic. "That would surprise me. You guys seem too young to be having heart attacks. But we can't take any chances. I'm calling 9-1-1. We need to get you to the emergency room right away."

Stan was less than enthusiastic about this idea so he blurted out, "Seriously? I don't really want to go. That's a real pain in the ass. Besides, I read that emergency rooms are getting overloaded in the pandemic. And I heard that just by being in an emergency room with other people I would probably catch the virus. Maybe I should just go home."

Larry was not about to let him off the hook. "No way. I've seen those stories, too. But if you are having a heart attack, the ER doctors are the ones who can treat you."

"Okay. Then can you take us in your car?"

Larry shook his head vigorously. "No way. I can't let the company assume liability for not getting you treated. None of us is a doctor, so the safest thing we can do right now is get you an ambulance. What if you have a heart attack in my car on the way? I'm not qualified to treat you."

Randy and Stan looked at each other uncomfortably but they realized that Larry was right. They had no choice. Larry was in charge. And secretly they were both actually relieved because they wanted to be taken care of.

When the EMTs got there about 15 minutes later, they strapped each man to a gurney and took them to the two ambulances. After both were loaded, the EMTs hooked them up to begin recording their pulse and breathing rate, blood pressure, and EKG. These vital signs were normal for both, but when the EMTs verbally quizzed them, they said that their discomfort had come on after they had gone into the computer equipment room. The EMTs weren't sure what significance it might have.

Neither Randy nor Stan had been in an ambulance before. Being the more outgoing of the two, Randy perked up like a little kid, totally forgot his concerns about ERs and COVID-19; he asked the EMT dozens of questions during the ride about the process and the monitoring equipment. The EMT gave him brief answers. When the ambulance pulled to the rear entrance of the hospital, Randy was struck by the irony of the situation. When the rear ambulance doors were opened, he could see that the ambulance had backed up to a low loading dock and to their left was a row of large trash containers. He asked the EMT, "Are you guys dumping me here with the rest of the garbage?" Randy thought his comment was hilarious, but apparently the EMT didn't. Maybe he had heard that dumb joke too many times. Randy and Stan were rolled into the ER on their gurneys. The emergency room was busy but not yet overwhelmed by COVID cases, so they were checked in quickly.

They were put through a series of diagnostic tests. Both had similar results: the Troponin test came back negative which, the doctors explained, indicated that no tissue damage had occurred in the heart. In both cases, doctors began to suspect that their symptoms were possibly due to anxiety. But, to be safe, and because they continued to complain of chest pain, they each were taken to have chest X-rays and MRIs.

The chest exams revealed mild buildup of fluids in the lungs and early signs of serious congestion in both cases, which explained their chest pain. Because Stan and Randy were exhibiting typical symptoms, the doctors ordered that they be tested for the COVID-19 virus. It turned out they were both negative. The doctors had no way of knowing at this point that they had been briefly exposed to hydrogen fluoride (HF) gas which had given them symptoms similar to COVID-19.

When HF gas comes into contact with moist areas like the eyes, nasal passage, throat, and lungs, it is converted to hydrogen fluoride acid and immediately damages the tissue. The degree of damage is determined by the concentration of the HF gas and the duration of exposure. Randy and Stan had only been breathing the HF gas for a few minutes, but that had been long enough to cause the pain and irritation they were feeling.

And even though they did not have the COVID-19 virus prior to this time, the damage to their tissues provided a fertile opportunity for them to be infected. And there were plenty of

COVID-19 viruses in the emergency room with patients coughing and hacking everywhere. So, both Randy and Stan quickly became infected. They were placed in hospital rooms so they could be observed overnight. The doctors were surprised to find that by the next morning both of them had significantly deteriorated.

The staff went into high gear and transferred them to intensive care where they could have access to more comprehensive treatment. By the next day, they were both on ventilators fighting for their lives. Prior to this hospital visit, they had been healthy young men with no underlying conditions, but unfortunately they continued to rapidly deteriorate. Clearly the ventilators were helping, but the congestion in their lungs was increasing at a horrendous pace and the doctors were having no success slowing down the progression of their infections. COVID-19 was ravaging their bodies at an accelerated pace.

Two days after being moved into the ICU, Randy died. Stan lasted a day longer, dying on the third day. Because such a large number of people were dying at the time, the doctors were somewhat puzzled by their rapid deterioration, but didn't have time to dwell on tracing the exact cause. It was the damage from that toxic gas that had made their bodies especially vulnerable to the virus, but the doctors didn't realize that.

PART VII

CHAPTER FORTY-THREE

APRIL 2020

The FBI team got another major break from Monica's visit to BizMoat Data Hosting Solutions. In the bottom of one the empty boxes, she found two intact cockroach specimens. At last, they had something to examine. These two cockroaches appeared to be dead, so Monica collected them and placed them into a plastic evidence bag and sent them via overnight delivery to the FBI lab.

The following day, Milton opened the package from Monica. Even though Milton knew that he was to receive a couple of bugs from Monica, he was still amused to see that the transparent evidence envelope really did contain two cockroach specimens. *What a strange case,* he thought. He was not an insect expert, but like many people who live in hot, humid areas, he was somewhat familiar with cockroaches. Based on their size—each was about two inches long—and their reddish-brown color, he deduced that they were the American cockroach variety *Periplaneta americana.*

He put on latex gloves and pulled the specimens from the envelope. They were dead but didn't seem to be particularly stiff or dried out, which seemed strange. The first simple step would be to place one onto a low-power binocular microscope to take a closer look. He made close-up views of the eyes, antennae, wings, and legs. Nothing remarkable came to mind. Then he flipped it over so he could view the ventral side. Again, nothing remarkable jumped out right away, but as he examined the ventral abdomen, he suddenly became aware that something didn't look quite right. In the midline, about halfway down the length of the abdomen, there was a small metal protrusion that looked like a hollow tube or needle. Milton swapped out the cockroach and placed the other one on the microscope's platform. He observed the same tube on that one as well.

"Hey, Alex, come over here and take a look at this. These cockroaches have little tubes stuck in their bellies."

Alexander Dobbins, another technician in the lab, strolled over to see what Milton was so animated about. After taking a close look himself, Alexander said, "So, they have tubes. What's the big deal? And, by the way, why are you looking at cockroaches?"

"Have you ever heard of insects with metal tubes in them? These were sent by Oakland Special Agent Monica Selden who says they are from a crime scene and may be significant."

Alex laughed out loud. "Okay, don't get mad. I was just asking. What do you plan to do with them?"

Milton was nonplussed. "Well, I'm not sure. I've never worked on anything like this. But she suspects they were involved in attacks on computers in Silicon Valley. I guess I should dissect one to see what's inside."

Alex smiled at his colleague. "Sure, makes sense. Now I'm curious, too."

Milton retrieved a scalpel, some pins, a small mounting board, some alcohol, and a couple pairs of forceps. He put the cockroach onto the board ventral side up, pinned it down, and made an incision along the center. He started at the thorax and continued straight along the entire length of the abdomen. To his utter astonishment, inside the thorax there seemed to be some mechanical parts. *This just gets stranger by the minute.*

When he reached the center of the abdomen, he hit something solid, fluid poured out, and it started to dissolve the tip of his scalpel as well as the bug itself. In a short time, the end of his scalpel was totally destroyed, as well as the cockroach.

The event took about twenty minutes and then the insect was reduced to a formless glob, resembling melted plastic, and the center of the mounting board under it was severely eroded as well. The fumes emanating from the melted specimen had a bitter pungent smell and burned his nose and eyes. Both of them jumped back and rushed over to the emergency faucets to rinse their eyes. It didn't take long for them to conclude that the acrid fumes were coming from some form of strong acid.

"Well, that was special," remarked Milton. "Clearly, when we dissect the other one, we'd better be extremely careful. We definitely need to take a look at it because before this first one dissolved, I saw some mechanical parts inside the thorax area. They seem to be artificial creations. Amazing. Let's move the dissecting tray over under the hoods to be safe."

Alex was fascinated. "That's incredible. I've heard that the military is working on small, autonomous drones that resemble insects, but I've never seen one. Do you think these are military?"

"Beats me. I've never seen anything like this either. I don't know why any military drones would show up at crime scenes."

"We better do a chemical analysis of the substance that dissolved the specimen."

Milton and Alex performed chemical tests on the cockroach remains and quickly determined that it was fluoroantimonic acid. Of course, Milton suspected that based on his previous work.

They moved the second cockroach under an exhaust hood and proceeded to carefully dissect it, avoiding rupturing the acid container. Inside the thorax they discovered the tiny circuit board, a small Lithium ion battery, and the piezoelectric actuators. From the head they found embedded photodiodes and some other tiny devices they weren't sure about. Later it would be determined that these were temperature and odor sensory modules.

Carefully working on the abdomen, they were able to tease around the small oval container in the center that they presumed contained the acid. This they handled carefully, removing it and placing it into a separate Teflon box for safety and analysis. The oval was located close to the metal tube that Milton had first observed, so the tube was probably some kind of release mechanism. Right now, he didn't want to find out the hard way.

Milton and Alex documented their analysis with extensive writeups and photos. They forwarded the report to their supervisor and sent copies to Monica.

What a trip!

CHAPTER FORTY-FOUR

Monica was working remotely from home when she received Milton's report, and she promptly forwarded it to Max and Jason before she opened the attached pdf file. Truthfully, she didn't know what to expect, but when she read the report, she was astounded. *Robot cockroaches?* It was unbelievable, and she had to reread the report to get past her amazement. She immediately called Max.

"Max, did you see the email I just sent you?"

"I saw it come into my inbox, but I haven't had time to read it yet."

Monica continued in a high-pitched excited tone. "You'd better open it up right away. You won't believe what the lab discovered about those two cockroach specimens."

Max opened up the attached report and read it in silence. He was having trouble digesting the contents of this report just as Monica had. His mind was flooded with ideas and theories. "This is incredible. Robot cockroaches? No wonder those cases have been so puzzling for us. It starts to make more sense now. That's why they were released at the target sites. They function as miniature weapons and probably are designed to self-destruct. And that's why the exterminators couldn't find evidence of actual cockroaches—these robots wouldn't behave like real cockroaches. They wouldn't be killed by poisons, for example. Has Jason seen this?"

"I forwarded it to him, but I don't know if he has."

As if on cue, Jason strode into Max's office with an astonished look on his face. "I just read the report. It's unbelievable. Like a science fiction movie."

Max replied, "Yes, it's pretty strange, but the report sure explains a lot. I've got to forward this to Tom. Now we know we're dealing with disgruntled cockroaches, not disgruntled employees."

Jason eyed him curiously. "Max, that's a pretty lame joke. But what do we do now?"

"We have to warn companies again about this immediately," Max declared, "so they don't keep accepting unordered boxes into their sites. Then we need to figure out how to track where these bugs are coming from. We need to stop any further shipments to company sites as soon as possible. Somebody must be creating these boxes and delivering them. I don't know for sure, but I assume they're local because all the attacks have been in the Bay Area."

Jason nodded. "That makes sense."

Max continued thinking out loud. "Ultimately, we need to track them back to their source. Where are they produced, and how do they get into the country? But, the first priority is to ward off any more attacks. The only thing I can think of is that we need to warn companies, but that will be tricky because I doubt we should go public with this. Can you imagine the panic that might cause?

"Monica, would you and Jason put together a plan? You should start by calling all the data center companies in the Bay Area and warning them about the possibility of receiving suspicious boxes. They should be concerned about any shipments that they are absolutely not sure that they ordered. They should hold any boxes they think are suspicious and turn them over to the FBI. I'm not sure what we'll do with them, but we need to get them off the street. And you should probably issue another more specific press release."

Monica spoke up from the speakerphone. "I'll get started right now."

"Thanks. I'm going to talk to Tom about how he wants to handle it. It's time to escalate this within the bureau. As far as tracking down the source of these packages, our latest targets should have information about who delivered the boxes. Those delivery services have records about the sender. Even if the sender's information is false, they still might be able to tell us where the package was picked up. That would be really helpful."

"That's a good point. Those data center companies would be a good place to start since we grabbed the boxes ourselves as evidence."

"Great idea. I'll get the tracking numbers from them right away. Then I'll start working backward in time to see what other boxes we can locate."

Max walked down the hall and strode into Tom's office without wasting time on preliminaries or jokes. "Tom, did you read that email?"

Tom looked up from his desk with a distracted and puzzled expression, "No, what's it about?"

Max sat down in the chair in front of Tom's desk. "I would prefer that you read it. You might think I'm pulling your chain."

Tom seemed preoccupied.

"You seem distracted. What's bothering you?"

Tom looked at Max and gathered his thoughts before responding, "Well, I've just spent about half an hour arguing with a Dean of Students at Stanford University. As you know, my son is a freshman there, and he's been told that all classes will be remote through the rest of the spring. I was arguing with him that we should get a refund on tuition. We're paying for the total college experience and not getting it."

Max was intrigued, but not having any kids of his own, he was unsure how to respond. "Did you get him to agree to a refund?"

Tom shook his head and simply said, "Fat chance. He kept trying to convince me that the remote experience would be just as valuable."

"So what are you going to do?"

"Well, I'll keep pestering the guy until I can squeeze a refund out of them. I hear that a group of Stanford students are circulating a petition asking for partial refunds for their tuition, and even their dorm fees and athletic fees. We'll see where that goes. I hear about similar petitions at other universities. I feel bad for the schools because it's not their fault, but we're talking about a lot of money, and I'm not a wealthy guy."

All Max could add was a lame comment. "Well, good luck. But I need you to read the email I just sent."

"Okay. Let me take a look."

Max waited while Tom scanned the email and attached file. Tom was completely shocked as Max had predicted he would be, and he appeared to read it multiple times before he looked up with a dumbfounded expression.

"When did you get this?"

"Just a short time ago. I forwarded it to you right away."

"Who else knows about this?"

"Besides the lab guys, just my team. But we need to decide who else to bring into the loop."

"Absolutely. What steps are you taking now?"

Max gave Tom a quick overview of the plan. "Ultimately, we need to figure out their origin, in other words where are they created and how do they get to the U.S."

Tom looked at him quizzically, "Do you think they are made here locally?"

Max shook his head vigorously. "I doubt it."

Tom was a bit surprised at Max's firm reply. "Why do you say that?"

"These are highly sophisticated little weapons. While the expertise surely exists here in the Silicon Valley, it seems pretty unlikely that you could hide an elaborate operation like this right under our noses. It would be too difficult to conceal, and rumors would leak pretty quickly; it's hard to keep secrets. My guess is that they are produced outside the U.S. and shipped here ready-made."

Tom was still pondering this possibility and asked, "By who?"

Max had been thinking about this ever since they had found out that the attacking devices were robots. "I don't have any proof, but this smells like our Chinese friends. They have the technology and production capabilities, and they are the ones who attacked us last year with those toy robots that started fires."

"Yes, but do you really think they'd be so bold as to try again?"

Max frowned. "Who knows. But don't be surprised if the trail leads back to China. Like I said, I don't have proof yet, but my team will pursue this investigation aggressively, and we will get the proof in time."

"Fine. I'll start alerting my superiors. You focus on the investigation. Keep me informed of any new developments."

"Will do." Max was relieved that the case was starting to break open after so many frustrating dead ends.

CHAPTER FORTY-FIVE

I t hadn't been much of a stretch for Max to reach the tentative conclusion that these robot cockroaches came from China. However, figuring out the exact origin was not as high a priority as intercepting shipments in transit to stop further attacks. Later, he could use the shipping information as a key source of evidence leading back to the source and to the local criminal actors.

Shipments from China came through the Port of Oakland that handled traffic from all over the world. Max called James Conway, the Port of Oakland Director, whom he had worked with on a previous case. That case involved the importation of remotely controlled robot toys that had been weaponized to catch fire once they reached target destinations in homes. An accidental warehouse fire at the Port of Oakland facility had provided key evidence for solving that previous case.

"Hello, this is Jim Conway. What can I do for you?"

Max was having trouble containing his enthusiasm that the case was seemingly starting to break for him. "Good morning, Jim. This is Special Agent Smart. You and I worked together last year on that big case involving toy robots imported from China. Thanks again for your assistance."

"Yes, I recall. No problem, I'm always happy to help."

Max got to the point quickly. "I appreciate that because I need your help again. We have an important case that has just taken a strange twist and I think it again involves shipments coming in through the Port of Oakland."

Jim was all ears. "Can you give me some details?"

Max paused to collect his thoughts. "The case is still evolving, but this latest information tells us that we need to act quickly." Then Max gave Jim a detailed overview of the attacks by the robot cockroaches.

Jim laughed out loud before responding incredulously. "Max, this sounds too strange to be true. Are you just pulling my leg?"

Max had actually expected this reaction. He assumed that to most people what he had just described would sound pretty farfetched. "No. I wish I was. This is serious. We need to stop these attacks as fast as possible."

Jim accepted his explanation and then got serious again. "What do you need from me?"

Max considered that for a brief second. "I don't have any proof yet, but my gut tells me that these robots are from China. It may even be the same perpetrators that mounted the attacks with the toy robots that you helped me with last year. I don't know. It doesn't really matter; what matters is that we cut off these attacks."

Jim could only agree. "Clearly."

Max was eager to get Jim started. "Search your manifests. First, can you identify shipments containing these robot cockroaches? They may use alternate descriptions to hide what they are, but I suspect they are labeled as toys of some kind like 'fake toy bugs' or anything that would allow them to pass customs." Max continued, "I will eventually need information to trace their origin, but right now I need to know the local destination. They may provide a false address, I don't know. But we should be able to track them down."

"That makes sense. I'll have someone in shipping and logistics start on this right away. Is there anything else?"

Max couldn't think of anything else at the moment. "I don't think so, though if there are shipments that fit my description, perhaps you could hold them up in customs so I can have agents follow any local deliveries in person."

Jim agreed that he could place a hold on any shipments. "I'll let you know. Let me get to work on this. I'll call you back as soon as I know something."

CHAPTER FORTY-SIX

Later that day, Jim called back. "Max, Jim here. I think we found some shipments that fit your description. Over the past five months, we have been getting weekly shipments from a company called Shenzhen Novelty Toy Export Company located near Guangzhou, China. The contents are listed as novelty toys—fake insects, specifically."

Max was elated. "Do you have any shipments there at the moment?"

Jim scanned the manifests again. "Yes. There are about fifty small boxes. What do you want me to do with them?"

Max stalled. "For now, I'd like you to find an excuse to hold them in the customs warehouse for a few days, so I can get my team organized. Whatever sounds reasonable to cause a delay."

"We can do that. Is two days enough time?"

Max was eager to find out a bit more. "Absolutely. I need to pull together a team so we can follow the shipment to the destination and nab these guys. By the way, do you have any information on who will be picking them up?"

Jim could be heard shuffling through some papers. "Looks like the majority of the previous shipments were picked up by a local delivery company called Northern California Express Freight in Alameda. We see them a lot here, mostly picking up smaller cargos for delivery to Bay Area destinations. They are a pretty small outfit with flashy red trucks."

Max made a note of the new information. "One more thing. Does the paperwork list the local address?"

Jim paused and Max could hear the paper shuffling. "No, it's blank. I assume that the delivery company has information that lists the address, don't you think?"

"Yes. I'll contact them next."

"Oh, Max, I just thought of one more thing that might be relevant."

"Go on."

"I noticed that there was about a two-month gap in ship-ments. "

Max wasn't surprised because it corresponded with the pause in attacks. "Thanks. Two months with no shipments. That's interesting. I saw in the paper that shipments in and out of the Port of Oakland are down considerably because of the COVID-19 crisis. Does it have anything to do with that?"

Jim pondered this question for a minute. "I don't think that's why because even though the overall volume is down, we've received continuous shipments from the Guangzhou Port, but none from this export company during the gap. I know they had factory closures all over China for a while. I suspect that was the cause. Max, I know you probably can't tell me right now because you're in the middle of your investigation, but promise me that you will call me later and let me know how it turned out."

"I will do that for sure. Thanks again for your help."

After Max hung up on Jim, he called the delivery company. His call was answered by a perky receptionist. "This is Northern California Express Freight the premiere delivery company in the Bay Area. How may I direct your call?"

"Please connect me to whoever is in charge. I'm FBI Special Agent Max Smart, and I need to speak with that person immediately." He was promptly transferred to Arnold Ledbetter, who had obviously been warned.

"Agent Smart, this is Arnold Ledbetter, the CEO. To what do I owe this surprise call? I'm not in trouble, am I?" he asked with a tense voice and a forced laugh.

Even a small company like this has a CEO? Sounds like an inflated title, but that wasn't really relevant.

"Hello, Arnold. No, you aren't in trouble, as far as I know." Max resisted the temptation to add a smartass comment like *yet.* No need to spook this guy. "I need some information regarding a few of your deliveries. You've picked up several shipments from the Port of Oakland coming from a Chinese company called Shenzhen Novelty Toy Company, and I need to know the specific address where they were delivered."

Arnold was relieved he wasn't in trouble. "That shouldn't be difficult. Let me contact our dispatcher. Let me put you on hold."

Max was feeling better about how the case was coming together. "Thanks. I'll wait."

Max was on hold for about five minutes. "Those shipments were delivered to Acme of China Toy Import Company. Their address is 1749 Demeter Street, East Palo Alto. The dispatcher told me we've been delivering packages to them for about four or five months. Apparently, it's a pretty new company, so we don't have a long history with them."

Max jotted down the information. "Thanks, that's just what I needed. Also, there's a shipment sitting in the customs warehouse. I've put a hold on it and the FBI will be seizing those boxes."

Arnold had actually already been worried about that shipment. "That solves a riddle for me. When I called to arrange pickup, the Port of Oakland informed me that my shipment was lost in their system."

Max was a bit alarmed. "Do you know if Acme of China Toy Imports is aware that there is a delay?"

"Not as far as I know. They haven't reached out to me about it."

Max wanted to keep a lid on the reason for the shipment delay. "Let's keep it that way. If they do call about the shipment, please just tell them that you don't know or that you'll check on it for them. And of course it goes without saying that you will not tell them about talking to the FBI. That must remain strictly between you and me."

Arnold was intrigued. "That sounds mysterious. Real cloak-and-dagger stuff. Can you tell me what's going on?"

Max wanted to close the door gently on Arnold. "Arnold, I know you are just trying to be clever and friendly, but this matter is serious. I can't tell you what's happening because we're in the middle of an active investigation." Max smiled and thought about the old stale joke, *If I told you then I would have to kill you.* "Just keep this to yourself. If all goes well, in a short time, what we're investigating will undoubtedly become public knowledge and then you will understand how important this matter is. Thanks for your cooperation."

Arnold felt a bit chastised. "Okay. I understand. I'll keep quiet and give them a quick excuse if they happen to call."

Max hung up on Arnold and then started planning for a raid on Acme of China Toy Importing Company. It needed to happen as fast as he could pull a plan together and execute it.

PART VIII

CHAPTER FORTY-SEVEN

I n the next day's team video call, Max updated the group. "Events are unfolding quite rapidly now that we've had a few breaks in the case. We discovered that the computer attacks were being done by robot cockroaches. We suspected that these devices originated in China, and we were right." He updated them on Acme toys and screen-shared his browser. "This is the Google street view of the front of their building on Demeter Street. It's part of a four-unit complex in a light industrial area, a modest one-story facility, which has just one front entrance and two windows. I don't have an image of the rear, but since it's on an alley, I assume that it probably has a rolling door and perhaps a loading dock for deliveries. Since this is not an end unit, it would seem that there are only two ways in and out—pretty easy to cover." He paused. "What I propose is a simple raid. A couple of you will station yourselves at the rear to make sure no one can exit from there. I'll approach the front door with Jason as the rest of you stand by. I'm not expecting this to turn violent, but you never know. I want to surprise them and move in quickly to seize evidence."

"What are you expecting to find?" asked Jason.

263

"I don't know for sure. Clearly, I'm hoping to find some of those cockroaches. But I also expect that we'll find evidence of how they're pulling off these attacks. I can't tell you what that is, but we must grab anything that looks suspicious in our raid—including computers, files, all of it. That's where the forensics team comes in."

"When do you want to do this? As you know, I have a problem with my kids being home from school," said Monica.

"I'd like to do the raid tomorrow morning. Can you arrange for that?"

Monica smiled lamely. "I'll check with my husband, but I can't guarantee anything yet."

Two other agents nodded indicating that they were in the same situation. Life had been upended by the pandemic. It had caught the nation by surprise and caused major disruptions. A new normal had temporarily taken hold with an unpredictable future.

Then Max thought of a possible solution. "Perhaps we can have you bring your kids into the office. We can set up a temporary area to use as a daycare center staffed by the admin people, or maybe we hire some outside daycare workers. It would only be for a day, or possibly only part of the day."

Everybody chuckled at the idea. It was clear that Max didn't have any kids. Bringing children into the FBI office would violate the social distancing guidelines—there was no way to keep the kids six feet apart for that length of time.

Monica spoke up for the group. "Max, that's creative, but it won't work. I think we can find babysitters at home."

"Great. Make it happen. I really need all of you."

After the video conference ended, Jason phoned Max to inform him that he'd tested positive for COVID-19.

"So what does that mean?"

Jason thought the answer was obvious to anyone remotely aware of the consequences of the COVID-19 pandemic, but responded simply, "In a nutshell, it means that I must quarantine myself for the next fourteen days. Hopefully, I won't get really sick, but there's no way to tell. And the rest of you might have been exposed so you need to get tested, especially if you develop symptoms."

Max was taken by surprise by this new revelation so all he could think was to ask a dumb question. "So can you help with the raid tomorrow?"

Jason was already overwhelmed by his positive results, so his patience was running thin. "I just told you, I'll be in quarantine —so no, I can't come."

Rather than admit he had asked a dumb question, Max simply said, "Okay. I'm sorry to hear about this. But I need to get off the phone, so I can call around to find a replacement. By the way, how are your parents?"

Jason hesitated. "Max, they're still sick, but they tell me they think they are improving. By far the hardest part is that I haven't been allowed to visit. And now I certainly won't be able to. We stay in touch with video calls and texts, but it's a poor substitute for actually seeing them in person."

Max was not sure how to respond. He said, sincerely but a bit lamely, "Okay. Best of luck. I hope they recover. And I hope that you don't get seriously ill. Let me know if you need anything."

Max hung up with Jason and made some quick calls to find a replacement. With just a few tries, he was able to line up Agent John Carter from the Oakland Office. Problem solved for now.

CHAPTER FORTY-EIGHT

Because of the social-distancing guidelines, the FBI agents drove to the Acme of China Toy Imports in separate cars. Fortunately, due to the lockdown, traffic was nonexistent, so none of them had trouble arriving on time. The COVID-19 rules might have to be bent during the raid. How do you hand-cuff a suspect from six feet away? There was no such thing as remote handcuffs. *If this was a science fiction movie, we could throw a forcefield around the suspects.*, Max thought.

As agreed, all of the FBI agents converged at Acme at nine AM in navy blue windbreakers with "FBI" printed in yellow block letters on the front and back. They were also wearing face masks, looking a bit like they were bandits from the Wild West. Two agents drove around to the back while Max and John Carter approached the front door. Monica and anoth-er agent stayed outside near their cars. Max strode up to the front door and knocked vigorously. A young woman opened the door. Before she could object, Max waved the search war-rant in front of her. As Max and John entered, Max asked if anyone else was present. As if on cue, a young man entered the front office from a back room. When he saw the FBI logo on their jackets, he stumbled and just about collapsed. The woman had turned pale as well.

Max announced that they were there to seize evidence and make arrests, so after he read them their rights, the two were instructed to stand to the side. Max called to Monica to send in the forensics team and told them to look for evidence.

The forensics team fanned out and began photographing the scene and collecting evidence. Everything was carefully catalogued, labeled, and placed into evidence containers. When they finished with the front office, the forensics team moved into the back room area where there were tables with a couple laser printers, a laptop, and some flat devices attached to power cords, apparently charging units.

There were ten small boxes stacked together in the corner. "Max, I think we found what we're looking for," Andrew shouted.

Before Max could respond, Andrew pulled out a pocket-knife and opened one of the boxes. As soon as he opened the flaps, an incredible swarm of cockroaches came shooting out of the box and scrambling in all directions. Some even darted toward the doors leading outside. They moved so fast that there was no hope of catching any of them. At least the agents remembered that the cockroaches were filled with dangerous acid, so they knew not to try to "kill" them by stepping on any.

Carter enthusiastically pulled out his revolver as if he thought he could shoot them. It didn't take long to realize how foolish that idea was. They were too small, too fast—impossible to hit with a 9-millimeter bullet. And shots fired could ricochet and hit any number of unintended targets. So he re-holstered his gun, but not before he looked at Max with a silly grin as if to apologize for his bad idea. All Max could do was to stare at him with disgust and shake his head.

Of course, it was too late to prevent the released cockroaches from traveling everywhere, but Max realized that he should have instructed the agents not to open any boxes. In a sense, it was useful because now they could observe firsthand how the robots operated. Unfortunately, now that they were free, they would start to damage equipment throughout the building. The other tenants would not be pleased. On one end of the building, the tenant was a cabinet-making business; on the other, there was a small auto repair business.

The forensics team was amused, until they realized the robots could cause a lot of destruction. Not to mention the poisonous gas. So, they decided to evacuate the other tenants. They prepared two large sealable containers to ship the boxes to Quantico.

The agents outside had seen some of the robot cockroaches scurry across the road and head for places unknown. Their first instincts had been to draw their weapons and shoot at them, but they also quickly realized that would be futile. All Max could think of was to have the agents warn businesses around the import company. *What a nightmare,* he thought.

A small number of local police had been asked to help with cordoning off the area around the raid. When they saw the FBI agents scurrying around after the cockroaches, they broke out in loud peals of laughter. It seemed especially comical to see the normally staid and serious agents scrambling around like a bunch of maniacs chasing the tiny "criminals."

Max turned to the two suspects and asked them to identify themselves. "John Chen" and "Debbie Wong" were the replies. After asking if they understood the rights that had been read to them, he asked several pointed questions, not really expecting any answers. Specifically, he asked why the robot cockroaches had been able to move out of the boxes. And what were they programmed to do? Could they be disabled or powered off to prevent damage? Obviously, John was scared stiff by the FBI and seemed eager to cooperate, undoubtedly hoping it would help him in the long run.

John began to blurt out a hurried explanation. "We use a wireless electric charger without removing them from the boxes. They aren't active until they're charged, and as long as the box is sealed, they're safe. They're programmed to attack computers and other electronic equipment. But they can't be shut down after they are loose. They are fully automatic and self-directed."

Max turned to the stacked boxes in the back of the room. "Great. So, the robots in those boxes back there are charged? *How* long can they operate?"

John's voice was gradually becoming higher. "Yes, we just finished charging them last night. They can operate for two to four hours, depending on how active they are. Charging them is one of the last steps before sending them out."

Max could only shake his head in amazement. "Wonderful. You don't charge them until you're ready to send them to a local site? I assume that once they're at a site that is to be attacked, they are primed to swarm out."

John was quick to respond. "Yes. We don't want them to be active before that. Especially during shipping." He almost betrayed a look of pride.

"How thoughtful of you," Max replied. John looked at Max curiously but didn't respond. Debbie remained silent and detached, seemingly lost in a private hell because it was sinking in that she'd been caught and was in deep trouble. Max turned to her with a few direct questions.

"Ms. Wong, what's your role here?" He expected her to remain mum, however she was just as intimidated as John, so she replied in a high-pitched and nervous tone. "I'm just an assistant. I help with receiving the shipments, creating address labels, taking the boxes to the delivery services. You know, basic admin tasks."

"In other words, you're just a gopher. A worker bee."

Debbie simply nodded.

Max stared at them pointedly. "You're both under arrest and shortly we will take you into the office for arraignment. We'll be interrogating you further because there's a lot more information that I need."

John couldn't help himself, and his anxiety got the better of him. He blurted out, "What will happen to us? What are the charges?"

Max paused to emphasize what he was about to say. "Suffice it to say you'll need to get yourself some good legal representation. I can't tell you all the charges you will face right now because the investigation is ongoing. But at a minimum, we'll charge you with terrorism, willful destruction of property, and reckless homicide. Perhaps we'll add importation of illegal substances, espionage, and tax evasion. You'll face a laundry list of criminal charges, and the jail time will be extensive."

It didn't seem possible, but John and Debbie became even more pallid as the color drained from their faces. John asked, "What do you mean reckless homicide? We didn't kill anyone. We only sent out these robots. I know they caused some damage, but nobody was murdered."

Max let out an audible sigh before responding, "Unfortunately, you are wrong. Two computer maintenance workers died after one of your attacks on a data center. Their deaths were caused directly by the attacks. That makes you culpable."

John looked shocked. "We didn't intend to harm anybody."

"That may be true. In the eyes of the law, it doesn't matter that you didn't *intend* to kill them. The fact of the matter is that they were killed as a result of a crime that you did intend, which makes you responsible for their deaths."

John and Debbie looked at each other, perhaps trying to enlist mutual support, but had nothing further to say. All they could do was look down at the floor. Mai would not get involved, so basically they were on their own and fundamentally screwed.

PART IX

CHAPTER FORTY-NINE

Mai dreaded having to make the call to the General. The project had totally failed. The FBI had raided Acme of China Toy Imports in East Palo Alto, California, and arrested her two agents. All shipments of robot cockroaches had been seized at the Port of Oakland and would be destroyed. Now that the project had been discovered by the FBI, no further attacks would be possible. Also, their American accomplices in the three data center attacks had been arrested and were to be charged with espionage and other crimes. And she had heard rumors that the Americans had traced the attacks back to China and were looking to place blame and perhaps ask for reparations. Without a doubt, the General would be absolutely furious that his project had unraveled. Knowing that the General would possibly react irrationally, she dialed his number with trepidation, though she was eager to get it over with.

The General was sitting quietly at his desk working through a stack of budgetary paperwork when he received the call from Mai. He listened to her update all the while growing increasingly angry, until he exploded over the phone with rage. "How could we this let this happen? I thought the project was going well. How did they figure it out?"

Mai didn't have all the answers yet, but she felt that she'd better offer some explanations, even if they were just guesses. "We think that the investigators found one of the robots at an attack site, and they figured out that it wasn't real. They were able to trace the origin of the shipments, which led them to Acme and then of course to the Port of Oakland, and that led them back to us. They raided the import company and got John and Debbie to confess and explain how the attacks were orchestrated. Apparently, once they figured out the cockroaches were robots, they were able to close in pretty quickly."

The General was quiet but fuming. He was leaning over his desk pounding on it with his fists. "This is unacceptable. How do we get restarted? Can't we set up another import company?"

Mai was surprised at what a dumb idea that was, but of course could not say that. "General, now that they know our method, I don't think setting up another company would work. They already know what to look for, so they'd block us immediately."

The General wouldn't admit it, but he immediately realized his idea was unworkable, so he responded by turning the responsibility back on her. "So, Mai, what do you think we should do now?"

She'd been thinking about this exact issue ever since she heard about the raid and arrests, so she was ready with an answer. "It seems to me that we must immediately shut down the factory, cease shipments, and destroy any evidence, including leftover drones, manufacturing equipment, and documentation. I'm assuming that our official position will be to deny any involvement."

Although it pained him to think about canceling everything, he knew it made sense. On the other hand, he wanted more clarification. "Are you suggesting that in addition to physical evidence we eliminate any people who were involved? Such as your team, or the executives at New China AI Creations?"

Mai did not know that after the General's failed secret Project Inferno, all the participants had been gruesomely executed. Nevertheless, she realized that she was treading on dangerous ground and needed to respond carefully. "No, General. I'm not suggesting that we actually, *ahem*, terminate anyone. In the case of my team, I think reassignment within MSS would be appropriate. In the case of New China AI Creations, I suggest that we inform them that the project is over, and that they stay silent about their involvement and destroy any implicating documentation. Same with Pangolin Electronics Manufacturing, who made the robots. They should be asked for an oath of silence, they should disperse their workers back into society, and the manufacturing facility should be dismantled." Mai let those thoughts sink in, then added an afterthought. "As far as John and Debbie, both are in custody in America, and we need deny any knowledge of their existence or connection to us. Unfortunately, they will be casualties, in a sense, but I see no other choice."

She hesitated to bring up the next topic, but she felt a strong urge to complete the story. "General, there's another reason we should distance ourselves. There was an unintended consequence of our attacks. Apparently, we had not accounted for the fact that the acid in the weapon emits a highly poisonous gas. At one of the data centers, two technicians were killed."

Rather than offer sympathy, the General just grunted and deflected her concern by saying, "I see. Is there anything else important I should know about?"

Mai wasn't sure how to respond to his lack of interest, but she didn't want to dwell on it either. "Not that I can think of right now. What do you want me to do?"

"Shut everything down. Do it immediately. All I want to hear back from you is that it's done." With that last comment, he slammed his phone down.

Mai was relieved to get off the phone. She pulled up her contact list and began making calls to the appropriate people, starting with the CEO of New China AI Creations. She thought to herself that in a way it would be pretty simple. Shutting down a project was certainly a lot easier than starting it up in the first place.

One more task had to be accomplished—she would need to enlist a set of MSS agents with security clearance to handle the destruction of Pangolin Electronics Manufacturing Company. That would take a considerable number of people, but she was confident that she would be able to enlist as many as necessary.

It took Mai the remainder of the day to tie up all the loose ends involved in shutting down the project. When she was done, she sat back and tried to relax, but she was still wound up from the collapse of the project. Now she had time to think about her own fate, which was uncertain at best.

CHAPTER FIFTY

MAY 2020

N ow that the plot had been uncovered, it was time to contact the Chinese government to make them aware of the accusations and demand that they desist and pay reparations. At the least, they needed to stop the program to prevent further damage to American companies. Tom gave the FBI director a thorough overview of the plot and a detailed description of how the local team had solved the crimes, and how the plot was now dead in its tracks. He also gave the director as much information as he could about how it traced back to China.

The FBI director had been updated about the ongoing investigation all along, but this was the first time he had a complete picture, and since the plot had been foiled it was time to involve other agencies. He contacted the State Department and explained the investigation. At first, State Department officials were skeptical because the whole story seemed too bizarre, and they couldn't understand the motive. But once the

FBI director detailed the evidence, including the corroborating information from John Chen and Debbie Wong, they believed him. After some short meetings and conference calls, the State Department concluded that they should bring the Chinese Ambassador in to meet in person with the Secretary of State, who would confront him directly with the evidence.

The Embassy of the People's Republic of China in Washington, D.C., is the primary residence of the Chinese ambassador. The Ambassador was not pleased when he was notified that the U.S. State Department demanded his presence at an emergency meeting. Though he didn't know what the subject might be, it still annoyed him that he had been summarily ordered to this meeting. He intentionally stalled for a few hours so as not to lose face.

When he arrived at the State Department offices in Foggy Bottom, he was escorted into a large conference room where he was confronted by the Secretary of State, some of the Secretary's staff, and the FBI director. As they looked up at the ambassador, their faces all clearly indicated that they were angry about something. The ambassador waited for them to take the lead because he knew he would find out soon enough.

The Secretary of State opened the meeting with a terse statement. "I'm going to dispense with any niceties and get right to the point. Your government has been conducting attacks on American companies since early this year. These attacks consist of a dastardly plot to attack and disable computer systems. These attacks are without precedent." He explained the extent and form of the attacks and waited for the ambassador to respond.

The ambassador was taken aback, and it showed on his face. He looked both shocked and perplexed and fidgeted nervously in his chair. After glancing around the room and obviously stalling for time, he finally responded, "These claims are ridiculous. The Chinese government has not conducted any such attacks."

The Secretary of State had been down this road before, and since he couldn't determine whether the ambassador's reaction was genuine, he just glared at him. "I expected you to deny these accusations. However, we have proof, and we have already taken the necessary steps to stop any further attacks."

The ambassador appeared to be stupefied. "What proof can you possibly have?"

The Secretary of State did not intend to provide details. "We don't want to reveal our information, nor our methods. However, we have undeniable proof that these activities were sponsored by the Chinese government."

Once again, the ambassador was speechless. This flood of accusations was too much for him to absorb in such a short time. "I don't believe that what you say is true. I categorically deny all accusations. However, that said, what do you want from me?"

"These attacks were directed by the Chinese Ministry of State Security in Guangzhou. You will inform your government in Beijing and tell them there can be no further attacks and that we will be seeking reparations for the damage."

"I understand. Even though the People's Republic of China has done none of these things that you allege, I will relay your concerns to Beijing."

The Secretary of State was satisfied that he had delivered his key points, so he wrapped up the discussion and dismissed the ambassador with a curt wave. "Thank you for your time, Ambassador. I expect an answer from your government within 48 hours."

Still shaken by what he had heard, the ambassador headed back to the embassy. The time difference between Washington and Beijing would make it difficult to contact the right people, however, this issue was so important that he would phone regardless. This was shaping up to be a diplomatic nightmare.

CHAPTER FIFTY-ONE

As soon as he returned to the embassy, the ambassador immediately began contacting government officials in Beijing. He started with his own superiors and told them they needed to engage Xi Jinping. "The Americans have accused China of sponsoring terrorist attacks against their citizens," he said, "using robot cockroaches that turned into weapons. They claim that there've been casualties and significant damage. I've been told that they are seeking reparations, but right now they want to know who is responsible, and how we plan to handle it."

They listened carefully and then patched in the Chinese president, who, after hearing the claims, said, "I find these accusations ridiculous. Is this a hoax? Do they have proof?"

"Yes, based on information provided by two agents in America who claimed they worked for the MSS in Guangzhou, they believe our government knowingly conducted this plot."

"What? That's impossible," exclaimed the president. "MSS wouldn't conduct an operation like this without my approval."

"They certainly shouldn't, but the Americans are convinced."

"Are the attacks ongoing?" Xi Jinping asked.

"The FBI claims to have stopped them."

"How do we get to the bottom of this? Regardless of what they say, our official line must be to deny any responsibility. But I demand to know who is responsible."

Xi reached over to the phone on the table and asked the operator to connect him to the head of the MSS. "I demand that you tell me about a secret program you are using to attack America... So you don't have a secret program that imports weapons into the U.S. to attack their companies?.... I hope that you're being truthful, otherwise the consequences will be dire.... Why wasn't I briefed?...."Obviously you miscalculated. This was not a minor project! It has exploded into a diplomatic fiasco. What do you intend to do about it?"

The ambassador listened to the president's side of the discussion. The head of the MSS patched in the General. "General, I need you to explain the covert program that you've been running and tell us its current status."

The General was not thrilled about this scrutiny from the officials. He preferred to stay in the background of the operation, but he complied. He provided them with a detailed summary of how it worked, its results, and how it had been discovered and blocked by the FBI. He quickly added a description of the steps that had been taken to bury any evidence within China. He was also careful to point out that the project had actually been approved.

President Xi listened carefully. "So you ran this operation under the cover of the COVID-19 crisis? Are you absolutely sure that all evidence has been removed? We do not need any more international criticism of our government."

The General wanted to make the president comfortable, so he reassured him as best he could. "Yes, we've destroyed the manufacturing and distribution facilities and any record of their existence. We have reassigned the MSS team members and sent the factory workers back to their villages. There's no evidence in China that would lead them back to us."

"That's what I wanted to hear. Our position will be complete denial."

After he hung up, the General thought, The shit's hitting the fan now. I'm glad I already had Mai tie everything up and cover our tracks.

PART X

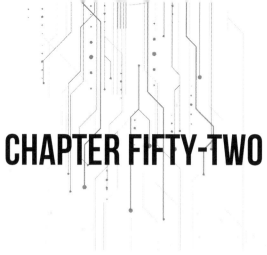

CHAPTER FIFTY-TWO

MAY 2020

Milton was sitting at his desk in the FBI lab sipping a mocha latte and staring at the sealed plastic container in front of him trying to figure out a plan to deal with the robot cockroaches inside. He had been provided with the lock combination, so opening it and taking out the two cardboard boxes was the easy part. The hard part was how to get them out without letting them destroy everything in the building.

The basic problem was that the robots would activate the moment they were freed. Containing them was absolutely critical. He built a plexiglas enclosure four feet square and four feet tall with a lid. The plan would be to dump them in and let them run around until their batteries died. Simple, really. You just had to assume that they couldn't crawl up the plexiglas, but even if they could, the lid would prevent them from escaping.

But Milton had not accounted for two factors. First, the cockroaches were extremely quick and agile. And second, he wasn't aware that their fake wing coverlets contained solar cells which could recharge their batteries.

After building the enclosure, Milton felt ready to proceed. He enlisted his co-worker Alex to place the lid on the enclosure since that required a second set of hands. Milton picked up one of the boxes, walked over to the enclosure, held it upside down, and used his pen knife to slice open the tape. Then he pulled a flap down and was rewarded with the spectacle of small brown insects tumbling out of the box onto the bottom of the enclosure. However, two of the robots were not fooled—they clung to the box and quickly crawled onto Milton's sleeve. "Holy shit! These fuckers are all over me!"

Fortunately, his reflexes kicked in; he brushed them off and they dropped into the enclosure. The entire time Alex was laughing hysterically; nevertheless, he managed to place the lid and seal the enclosure. On the bottom, the robot cockroaches were scrambling in all directions, crawling over each other, maniacally seeking to escape, and making a horrendous scratching sound. Some tried to crawl up the sides but were only able to make it about six inches before falling back. It was eerie watching them in action because they looked so real. Milton had to remind himself that they were not real.

Since he'd been told that their batteries could last up to four hours, there was no point in waiting. That would be like watching paint dry. So he left for the day and turned off the lights on his way out. The next morning, he arrived early, eager to get started. He walked over and looked into the enclosure, and sure enough the robots were laying inert on the bottom. No movement at all. Milton went over to the other side of the lab to set up the new portable X-ray probe he'd purchased to capture digital images showing their internal structure without cutting them open.

He was stalling because frankly there was a part of him that was a bit frightened by these fake bugs. But after a short while, he walked back over to the enclosure to take one out, which is when he noticed something peculiar. About half the robots had oriented themselves parallel to each other, with their dorsal sides facing up in the same general direction towards the overhead lights. *Of course they have a way to recharge. Why didn't I think of that before? Lucky for me, I haven't removed any of them yet.*

He tested his theory by placing a bright desk lamp to one side of the enclosure. Sure enough, most of them slowly reoriented themselves to hold their wings perpendicular to the light source. *Now what do I do?*

Milton decided he'd need to keep the enclosure in a dark place, remove a few at a time after they were dormant again, and quickly cut off their wings to disconnect the solar cells. Only then would they be safely disabled.

The next day, he put his new plan into action and had two specimens to work with under his portable X-ray probe. He had gotten the idea for using a portable X-ray probe after visiting his dentist. The device was compact and totally self-contained, and it produced hi-resolution images, which showed their complex construction. Some of the components were easily identifiable, such as the circuit board, the battery, and the acid pellet. But many of the components were mysterious. He compiled a report with images from all angles, and he added the chemical analysis information to round it out.

Milton had been told to expect some visitors from the Pentagon. They were extremely interested in exploring the cockroach technology for covert surveillance or weapons development. Milton was looking forward to that meeting, and he was sure the military guys would be impressed. He was certain that these creations would find a home somewhere in the arsenal of the U.S. military establishment.

PART XI

CHAPTER FIFTY-THREE

The General sat behind his massive wooden desk staring out the window at the Guangzhou cityscape lost in thought and still fuming about his project's failure. In the distance, he could see thunderstorms brewing in the distance. His idle thoughts were interrupted by an announcement from his secretary informing him of a visitor—his superior at the MSS.

As Ming Quon, the head of MSS, emerged from the left side of the feng shui partition, the General looked up at him and forced a smile. "This is an unexpected surprise. To what do I owe this visit?"

Ming walked over to take a seat in front of the desk opposite the General. He appeared to be agitated, he fidgeted in the chair, and was having difficulty looking directly at the General. Obviously, he was annoyed about something. At last, the uncomfortable pause ended. "Your latest sabotage project has unraveled and been shut down by the FBI. Your local agents have been arrested and your robots seized. Worse yet, the Americans are blaming China and threatening diplomatic action. This is unacceptable."

The General was still angry, and he replied with a touch of sarcasm. "I don't need to be reminded or lectured to. I'm well aware of the situation."

Ming was warming up to his uncomfortable task. "I'm sure you're embarrassed by your failure, but I didn't come here to rub it in. I came to tell you what we're going to do about it."

The General didn't like where the conversation was headed, so he made an effort to calm himself before responding. "What does that mean? What *are* we going to do about it?"

Ming just wanted to get to the solution. "It's simple. You will retire from MSS. Immediately. No option."

The General was taken by surprise. He thought that he'd be forced to take a demotion, perhaps a public reprimand, but not a forced retirement. "I'm not ready. I was planning to stay here for several more years."

Ming frowned, nodded his head a few times, then replied, "This is not optional." To soften the blow, he added, "You will be given a stipend. And you might actually enjoy retirement. You are still relatively young, and nobody wants to work forever. We all have to retire at some point."

The General was not sold on these arguments, but he knew that he'd have to accept the conditions regardless of how he felt. He also knew that it could be a lot worse. He realized that they could just "retire" him permanently with bullet to the head, or some more creative death. Walking out the door with his health intact was preferable. "When would I have to retire?"

Ming was pleased that the General seemed to accept the situation. "I would like you to evacuate your office by the end of the week."

The General's head was spinning. "What should I tell my people?"

Ming looked at him pointedly. "Nothing. Let me handle that. We'll just announce that after a long and successful career with MSS, you've decided to move up the date for your long-planned retirement. We will make it sound like a logical choice."

"But almost everyone will know that I've been forced out."

"Of course that's a possibility, but there isn't anything to be done about that. People will have a variety of opinions, none of which we can control."

The General was not pleased by this response. But he would just have to deal with the fallout as best he could. Since they were old friends who'd worked together for many years, Ming said with a sympathetic tone, "I know this is sudden, but what do you think you will do?"

The General turned to look out the window and paused to gather his thoughts. "I'm not sure. Obviously, it would have been better to have time to plan. My first thought is that I will relocate. I inherited a villa on Hainan Island, perhaps I'll move there. I just don't know. I need some time to think."

Ming tried to keep any cynicism out of his voice. "That sounds like a good plan. Let me know if there's any way MSS can assist with your relocation."

The sarcasm was not lost on the General, as hard as Ming had tried to hide it, but he did not reply.

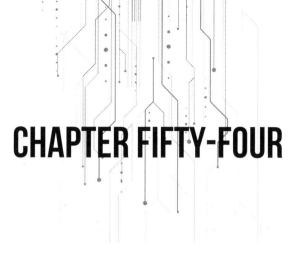

CHAPTER FIFTY-FOUR

O n a balmy afternoon in July, the General was taking his daily early evening stroll along the sandy beach near his villa in the Tianya District neighborhood of Sanya on Hainan Island. Getting out on the beach for a stroll was one of his favorite activities, and he usually enjoyed it most in the early evening as the sun was setting over the South China Sea. Most of his colleagues knew the General as a hard-nosed, even brutal, official in the MSS, so it would come as a great surprise to discover that he had an artistic side. He was an ardent photographer, and he possessed a profound appreciation for color, lighting, patterns, and composition. Dusk is a cherished moment for photographers because the light becomes softer, and the low angle of the sun illuminates objects in a special way, making them more distinctive and interesting.

For example, as he gazed to his left, he could see the five towers of the new resorts on Phoenix Island gleaming as the setting sun glinted off their modern steel-and-glass architecture. After dark, these towers would light up with multicolored floodlights. Just to the left of the towers, the white high-rise buildings of downtown Sanya were highlighted by the setting sun and shone in the distance. The view was framed by a seemingly endless line of dark-green coconut palms running along the back of the gently sloping beach. He was always entranced by the contrast of the hues. The greenery of the coconut palms juxtaposed with the white sandy beach, the green-blue water, blue sky, and white and silver buildings.

Gazing southward to the open sea, he could see two small islands about two miles offshore. Xidao Island, about a half-mile long with a low hill in the center, has a small number of modest homes and two hotels, and about half of the island was set aside as a nature reserve. The much smaller Dongdao Island, only three tenths of a mile long, is mainly unoccupied, save for a government facility in the center, probably military, but the General didn't know.

Turning to his right, the General had a view of another seemingly endless stretch of white sand beach bordered by graceful coconut palms tilted toward the ocean. This western part of Sanya was primarily residential, so there were no high rises poking up above the trees, just numerous two- and three-story condos and resorts that were proliferating in his neighborhood. As he soaked up this view, which included the setting sun on the horizon, the silence was disrupted by the roar of a passenger jet taking off from the Phoenix Sanya ational Airport a few miles to the north. There were a few people on the beach but most of the tourists had retired for the day.

Looking back again at the vast South China Sea, he was suddenly aware of the pleasant salty odor wafting in on a soft breeze. He was bathed in the bright rays of the setting sun, and he was struck by the colors of the sand, trees, and ocean around him. But in the distance, there was a band of black clouds that looked like a descending curtain. According to the forecast, the typhoon would hit in two days, so he was observing the early signs of its approach. He had heard that it might be quite destructive, but the exact landfall was still unknown, so perhaps his villa would be spared. At any rate, he would remind his staff to prepare the villa to protect it. Typhoons were a regular nuisance in the rainy season, but it was never wise to take them for granted.

The General was startled by the vibrations of his phone in his shirt pocket. He was surprised to see a text from Ming Quon, head of MSS, who was vacationing in Sanya and wished to stop by for a visit. That seemed odd to the General, since he'd only recently seen his colleague upon learning of his force retirement. At the time, Ming hadn't said anything about a vacation on Hainan Island. The General responded with a dinner invitation for the following evening and began the short walk back to his villa across the frontage road.

As he strolled down the path through the grove of coco-nut palms, he saw the four agents who'd been assigned to protect him. They did their best to stay discreet, but based on their tendency to lift their wrists up to their mouths and speak, it would be pretty obvious to about any observer who they were. Actually, it probably was probably best that they were identifiable because that alone would deter people from ap-proaching the General.

He walked up the flower-lined pathway to the front of his villa and stepped through the solid wood door where he had to detour around the feng shui barrier just inside. Many people erected barriers like paneled folding screens, but in this case, there was a solid interior wall that faced visitors as they entered the foyer. The superstition held that these barri-ers would block evil spirits from entering the house, and the General was an avid believer.

He strolled to the sideboard and mixed himself a rum cocktail, then sat down in a traditional Chinese-style wooden chair that faced the interior atrium of the house. This living room was lavishly appointed with fine wooden furniture and traditional sculptures, mainly of animals and beautiful Chinese vases. The walls were painted light blue with large paintings on two sides, primarily of traditional landscapes. The house had been in his family for years, and it gave him great com-fort to be there. His father had been an officer in the Chinese Communist Army that captured Hainan Island in 1950 and ejected the Chinese nationalists thus bringing Hainan back as a province under mainland Communist China. The General's rise within MSS was assisted by his father's reputation within the Party.

His father had purchased the villa and remained on the island as a local government official until his death in 2001. Though the villa was comfortable, it also held many bitter-sweet memories. He had grown up there until he moved away for university, and he used to bring his family for vacations when they were still alive.

So, when the General was told that he needed to retire, it was natural that he would relocate here from Guangzhou. He was provided a yearly stipend that, when combined with his investments and his savings, was more than adequate. He treated himself to two luxuries—a gardener, Fei Hong, to care for his grounds and atrium, and a housekeeper, Zhi Ruo, to cook and maintain the household. Both of them had worked for the family for many years, so he was used to having them around, and they were companions as well.

In addition to the four security agents provided by MSS, the interior and exterior of the villa was outfitted with an elaborate video surveillance system, monitored 24/7 from a dedicated control room in one of the outbuildings. As far as the General was aware, there were no immanent threats, but considering his long career at MSS, his old associates thought it was only prudent to assign high security just in case.

He thought about his friend's visit scheduled for the next day and decided he should make it special. He called out to Zhi Ruo, knowing she was usually hovering just out of sight. He looked up as she entered the living room. She was an old, diminutive woman, thin with gray hair, and she was wearing a floral red collarless, long-sleeved overcoat and black silk slacks. She was at least as old as the General, probably older, but he didn't know for sure. However, she had worked for the family since he was a boy, so maybe she was even older than he imagined. He also noticed that she was growing increasingly thin and frail with time.

"What can I do to help you?" she asked, smiling warmly.

The General smiled back. "I have a simple request. My old boss and friend from MSS, Ming Quon, is visiting tomorrow evening. I would like you to prepare that exquisite dish you've made so many times, Wenchang chicken. It's my favorite, and I know my friend would love it as well."

"That will be easy. What time will he arrive?"

"I'm not certain, but let's assume six p.m."

"I will have it ready. What else would you like to go with the dinner?"

"How about plum wine and fresh fruit, especially pineapple, and coconut pudding?"

"I will see to it."

"Thank you."

The General turned to gaze through the large plate-glass windows facing the atrium, nursing his cocktail. *After the typhoon passes,* he thought, *I need to have Fei Hong trim those hibiscus bushes on the far side.*

CHAPTER FIFTY-FIVE

The following evening, Ming Quon arrived at the front door. It was pouring rain as the outer bands of the typhoon approached Hainan. Even though the guards had been notified of his pending visit, they still carefully checked his credentials and then allowed Ming into the house.

The General greeted his old friend warmly and ushered him into the dining room where the table was already set for a formal dinner. The General had asked Zhi to set the table with the China plates from his family's heirloom collection, expensive enamel-coated chopsticks, and fine crystal wine and water glasses. Ming had arrived carrying a leather briefcase from which he pulled a bottle of wine and handed it to the General.

"It's good to see you again, old friend," said Ming continued. "How are you enjoying retirement?"

The General accepted the wine, looked down at it without recognizing the label, got a distant look in his eye, and responded. "As you know, I wasn't ready to retire, but now that I'm here, it's working out. I'm lucky that I have this villa, so the change hasn't been a total shock. It's quieter and less hectic than Guangzhou, and less polluted. I enjoy the tropical climate and the beauty of the place, too."

Ming looked at him with genuine interest. "Tell me, what do you do with your time?"

The General got an almost whimsical look. "A variety of things. Almost every day, unless it's raining, I take a walk down to the beach to watch the sunset. I indulge my hobby of photography. And I'm sure you never knew this, but I'm an avid bird watcher and there are plenty of nature reserves where I can indulge in that pastime. I'm also thinking about taking up golf, and perhaps going to the local casinos, but I'm not sure about that because I hate to lose money."

Ming chuckled at that last comment and nodded. "I'm glad to hear you're keeping busy. And you're right. Obviously our friendship has been mainly professional because I did not know about your hobbies. It's fortunate that you have them, many retired people are hard-pressed to find useful things to do."

The General nodded and smiled with a knowing look.

Ming abruptly changed the topic. "I brought this fine wine. Let's toast to your happy retirement. But let me use the bathroom quickly before we do that." He set the wine bottle on the table and left the room. The bathroom was just down the hallway, and once he was out of sight, he swallowed four large, activated-charcoal tablets. These would absorb the aconite poison he had placed in the wine that they were about to drink. Aconite, also known as monkshood or wolfsbane, is extremely poisonous, but the charcoal would protect him. Ming was deeply regretful that he was about to poison his old colleague, but he believed it was necessary because the General harbored too many secrets, some of which could come back to haunt Ming.

However, after he sat down and stared across the table at his old friend, Ming realized that he could not go through with it. After all, the General was an old friend who deep down Ming did not wish to kill. Also, the General was an old hand at dealing with secrets, so it was probably too paranoid to think that he might be indiscreet. And Ming was forming a vague thought in his mind that the General might be useful again in the future. For what, he didn't really know—it was just an intuition.

Ming walked back to the table, sat down, and resumed the conversation. He made a great show of reaching for the bottle but clumsily knocked it off the table onto the hard marble tiles where it shattered and splashed bright red across the floor. Ming stood from the table. "What an idiot. I can't believe I did that. I'm sorry for creating this mess." The irony was of course lost on the General who had no idea that his life had just been spared.

The MSS agents in the other room had heard the crash and rushed into the room. Ming took advantage of their confusion by loudly proclaiming his clumsiness. Zhi entered the room. Upon seeing the broken glass and big puddle of wine, she muttered a few choice curse words, and then left to get some cleaning supplies.

Ming sat down quickly as if he was worried about fainting, covered his face with his hands, and continued to issue apologies interspersed with comments like, "I'm such an idiot. What a stupid peasant I am." It was quite the performance, though in truth, Ming actually was deeply relieved for not carrying through his original plan. But it was over, so he could relax. The evidence of his planned treachery would disappear once Zhi finished removing the broken glass and spilled wine, and that would be the end of it. Since nobody had actually been poisoned, there would be no reason to test the wine for a poison. Time to move on.

The General had Zhi bring in a new bottle of wine from his own cellar, and he and Ming continued their dinner and conversation. Two bottles of wine later, Ming made his excuses and left for Beijing. Neither of them knew at the time, but their fates would intersect again in the near future.

CHAPTER FIFTY-SIX

JULY 2020

Max was gazing out the window of his office in Oakland at his favorite view pondering the COVID-19 pandemic and how it had impacted his life. Not only had the pandemic interfered with his sabotage investigation, a small thing in the big picture, it was a problem with no end. Just a frustrating situation that would continue to screw up people's lives for years to come.

Jason and Monica wandered into Max's office and took a seat across the desk from him. Monica set a mocha from Starbucks on his desk. "We thought you needed a coffee break. Here's your favorite."

Max smiled and grabbed the coffee, not sure how he was going to be able to drink it since he was wearing a mask. They all laughed out loud at the situation. Monica suggested a solution. "Let's slide our chairs back so we're further apart. Then we can take our masks off while we drink our coffee."

Over coffee, Max said, "We raided the import company about two months ago—what's the status of the two suspects, Chen and Wong?"

Jason and Monica looked briefly at each other, then Jason spoke up. "They're both in custody at the Federal Building. My understanding is that they've been abandoned by the Chinese. They haven't been helped with bail. They're using public defenders because they can't afford lawyers. I heard that their lawyers were working on a plea deal, but I don't think the District Attorney is eager to cut any deals. Right now, both of them are facing the possibility of a long time in federal prison."

Max nodded. "Believe it or not, I hope they get reduced charges. They deserve to be punished—no way can we condone what they did—but they were nice kids, just low-level players, and I don't wish them ill will. I'll never forget the horrified look on their faces when I told them about the two techs who died. I don't think they intended to hurt anyone. Nevertheless, they do need to be punished, and I will leave that up to the District Attorneys and the court to decide."

Monica added, "I agree. When we busted them in the raid, my first impression was that they were just a couple stray puppies. Clearly, they were in way over their heads. They sure provided us with lots of useful information and evidence."

"Jason," Max started, "have you heard from your contacts within the State Department? Have they identified who's responsible?"

"Well, they are being pretty tight-lipped about it. They're trying to snow me into thinking that the matter is too sensitive for me, but the truth is that they haven't been successful, and they just don't want to admit it. It sounds like just what we predicted. That is, the Chinese government has denied knowledge of any plot. They called it 'fake news.'"

Max actually laughed out loud. "They are quick learners."

After he got the laughs out, Max resumed his questioning. "As I recall, we traced the shipments back to a toy exporter in Gaungzhou. Do we know anything about them?"

Jason explained, "As you know, it is difficult to dig up intelligence within China, but what we did find is that that particular company no longer exists. Totally shut down and removed from databases as well. It was probably just a passthrough entity."

Max laughed as the story was playing out just as he'd expected. "All the signs of a classic cover-up, which means the Chinese government did know about the plot."

Jason nodded. "Another piece of the cover-up seems to be the complete disappearance of the factory, Pangolin Electronics, which we believe was where the cockroaches were assembled. Our covert agents went to that location, and it simply does not exist. They scrubbed out all traces of it. Clean slate."

Max could only smile. "At least we know they're thorough. What happened to the factory workers?"

"Since most of them were probably young women from the countryside, we think they were just sent back to their villages and told to forget what they'd seen."

"I guess in the big picture that makes sense," said Max. "The Chinese government will deny the plot, and after all, who would believe a peasant girl with a wild story?"

Jason had an afterthought. "We did glean one other tidbit, but it may be a coincidence. A bigshot in MSS, Liang Xoabai, also known as 'the General,' suddenly retired and moved to a tropical Island. It's possible that he was removed. Maybe it was a reward for running the plot, since we have reason to believe he was in charge."

Max took this in. "Interesting. Coincidences take a lot of planning. I bet the General was involved in the sabotage, but we will probably never know for sure." He sat back with an audible sigh and turned to look out the window at the beautiful San Francisco Bay. He really hoped that the General's retirement might bring on his own. Of course, he couldn't prove that the General had been responsible for directing the two plots he'd solved in the past year, but the connection was clear to Max.

At any rate, staring at the graceful sailboats on the bay re-inforced his desire to retire and get out from under his stress-ful job. Max didn't actually know how to sail, but he figured that learning would be a lot easier and more enjoyable than chasing bad guys.

THE END

EPILOGUE

DECEMBER 2020

Jason had recovered from his infection, though it took about a month, and he said that it was like the worst possible flu he could imagine. His parents had also recovered, but a new rise in cases was occurring in nursing homes, and Jason was worried that his parents might be reinfected. Monica was still saddled with the dual responsibilities of home-schooling her children because the schools were not scheduled to reopen; perhaps not until the following school year. So far, Max had managed to avoid getting infected. However, with COVID-19 spreading rapidly, he was gradually becoming resigned to the idea that it was only a matter of time before he caught the virus. The way he looked at it, it was simply a numbers game. As more people were infected, the chance of running into an infected person would just keep rising. Also because of the strain on ICU facilities, he had to postpone his back surgery again, and it wasn't clear when he'd be able to reschedule it—soon, he hoped.

Vaccines for COVID-19 were about to roll out nationwide, and by the middle of 2021, most Americans would be able to be vaccinated. That was certainly good news and would eventually control the outbreak. Of course, that would depend on how many were willing to take it—an open issue. Frantic efforts were underway to develop therapeutics to treat infected people and several were showing promise.

Still, most Americans found it difficult to grasp how widespread and devastating the COVID-19 pandemic had been and understanding how long-lasting it would be. Beginning in March with the initial shutdown, the economy had been gutted. Over 45 million people were unemployed. Revenue for many industries plummeted. In particular, the travel and hospitality industries were hard hit. At one point, airline travel had dropped 95% and the same dreadful drop occurred for hotels, car rental companies, and restaurants. Service industries, such as hairdressers, barbers, manicurists, and others, had to close their businesses. People literally stopped traveling, so gas sales fell precipitously. Further, the decline in tax revenues that resulted from these business closures would have far-reaching consequences for state and local governments—they'd be forced to cut programs and lay off workers before long.

So, there was a lot of political pressure to "reopen" the economy, which resulted in the lifting of restrictions in May. However, less than a month after restrictions were lifted, the number of COVID-19 cases began a sharp rise that accelerated to a peak in mid-summer. Most experts just described this as a continuation of the first wave of the virus.

Based on wishful thinking, pundits were predicting that as soon as the nation opened up, it would immediately enter a V-shaped economic recovery, meaning that it would take off like a rocket ship and get back to pre-pandemic levels. At the same time, others predicted that a wave of bankruptcies would happen in early 2021 in small and large businesses, as well as in the real estate markets as many homeowners, renters, and landlords would be unable to make their monthly payments.

And of course, consumer spending had fallen drastically with no expectation that people would want to spend freely again. Thus, the economy would be slow to recover. Online sales rose dramatically as people avoided stores. Curiously, sales of used autos soared and prices shot up about 30%. Apparently, many people wanted to avoid public transportation and were looking for a reasonable alternative. Some economists are of the opinion that a full recovery will probably take five to ten years, a timeline that's more consistent with major recessions of the past.

And unfortunately, these optimistic predictions don't account for the impact of possible additional waves of the virus. Many optimists stated that the second wave would come in the fall and winter when the virus might peak and then fade away. Unfortunately, COVID-19 did not wait. It simply thrives on targets—meaning us. And it is highly opportunistic and contagious. The lifting of earlier restrictions along with the naive belief that the virus was in the rearview mirror caused some to assume that the problem was solved so there was no need to be careful. This attitude was visible in the parties and celebrations that occurred around the holidays.

Other situations contributed to the surges. One was a series of events that nobody would have predicted. As a reaction to the murder of George Floyd in Minneapolis, the entire country was roiled by over three weeks of massive protests, drawing extremely large crowds. And even though many of the protesters showed up with face masks, they were often in close contact. One doctor was quoted as calling the protests "a smorgasbord for COVID-19," while another pundit simply said, "the virus is marching with you." Not long after the protests, the nation endured a huge wave of new cases which would complicate any prospects for a quick economic recovery.

Also, predictably, the Labor Day weekend with its large gatherings and parties around the country drove another spike in cases. About the same time colleges and universities reopened and in spite of their best efforts to follow the CDC guidelines, many of them became large outbreak sites.

In addition, many Americans chose to travel widely over the Thanksgiving holiday that contributed to another surge. A surge on top of a surge, as the CDC put it. And the prediction was that Christmas travel and New Year's Eve celebrations would create similar surges.

As of December 2020, COVID-19 cases and deaths were once again rising at a terrible pace, surpassing the peak levels from the summer spike. Nationwide there were over 15 million cases and nearly 300,000 deaths. In California alone, there were about 1.4 million cases and over 20,000 deaths. By mid-December, the number of cases was rising by 30,000 per day with no end in sight. As a result, on December 7, 2020, California put in place another lockdown intended to last until January 4, 2021, but with no guarantee that it would be lifted. Time would tell.

This virus is relentless. The vaccines will help, but they won't be widely available until the middle of 2021 so in the meantime the pandemic will continue to rage. Unfortunately, experts have predicted that the worst is yet to come; COVID-19 will be with us for a long time.

ABOUT THE AUTHOR

William W. King (Bill) has been retired for eleven years following a 10-year career as a teacher in higher education, and a 25-year career as a systems engineer in telecommunications. He currently resides in Los Altos, California.

Made in the USA
Monee, IL
16 September 2021

0050c515-5e35-4a5a-8046-a795284dc605R01